MY CREATOR

I am aware that *Grace* was only made possible because of the gifts,
talents, experiences, people and unshakable faith
gifted to me by my Creator.
I believe with all my heart and soul that *Grace*,
the little masterpiece that you now hold in your hands,
was co-created by "The One" who gifts grace to us all.

CONTENTS

PROLOGUE

I t was said that "The Book" would be found in darkest space; in a void where all possibilities exist. It was waiting there to be created. Waiting for "the one" to imagine it into reality.

A talisman to be passed from age to age, from mother to daughter and from father to son, an institute for the generations still to come. "The Book" contained "The Key", The Key that unlocks all of Creation and the heart of The Universe itself.

A precious treasure, "The Book" had been desired by many. But even those who had held it in their hand could not see the power that lay within, for it was the simplicity of its message that fooled them, and their chosen unbelief.

But a child could see it. A child-like heart would understand its simple message.

Like a tiny Alice in Wonderland, Grace stood in front of the enormous door. It was locked. She banged on the wood in frustration. She was crying, inconsolable sobs shook her body. Giving the door one final, desperate strike, she *Asked*.

As the door slowly opened Grace saw "The Book" for the first time. It was glowing, a radiant light that became stronger and stronger. She stood captivated. Her eyes widened as she noticed letters materialise on its front cover, written in gold by an invisible author. She read the word aloud. With her heart pounding in her chest she closed her eyes, looked up to the heavens and gave thanks.

Grace now understood the meaning of *the word*.

CHAPTER 1

THE OLD LADY

Grace woke up and immediately felt reluctant to get out of bed. It was 9.08am. She should have been up well over an hour before that, but as usual, struggled to find the energy to start her day. It had been like that for a long time. As long as she could remember.

She lay staring at the ceiling, thinking. Hundreds of thoughts raced through her mind. Anxiety gripped her, a vice like tightness spread across her chest. Grace pulled the duvet cover over her head. She felt safe and protected under there, curled up in the dark and away from the world.

She knew that once she emerged, that would be her, non-stop, all day and night until the early hours of the following morning when she would have to practically extract herself from her laptop. Project deadlines, trying to control everything; a symptom of her own perfectionism, all kept her held in an unrelenting cycle that wasn't doing her any good. She knew it, but couldn't work out how to make the changes she needed to.

Finally surfacing, she dragged herself up and out of bed and moved across the room to check her diary. Grace glanced down at the page. It was Monday. The diary entry read "The Key." Great start to the week. An interview with a positive thinking "guru", the woman who was energising the city with her personal development programme. 'This should be interesting!' Grace was sceptical. 'I'd like to see her work her magic on me!'

Grace moved round the house, picking up items of clothing from the floor, mumbling to herself about becoming more organised as she dressed. She grabbed a cup of coffee and a breakfast cereal bar then made her way out of her flat and into her car. She put the key in the ignition and turned it, the car jolted forward and stopped dead. She turned the key again and again. Nothing. She looked around for help from a neighbour, a passer-by, anyone, but the street was deserted; apart from a lone magpie which had landed a few feet away. Banging the steering wheel in frustration, Grace looked at her tired eyes in the mirror, sighed hopelessly and said 'Why me?'

She pushed the door of her little champagne coloured Mini open, leapt out and slammed it angrily behind her. She walked quickly down the road to the nearest bus stop and waited for what seemed like forever. She could feel her chest tightening and pulse tapping against her temples.

'At last!' she moaned under her breath when the bus arrived. Grace jumped on ignoring the driver, paid her fare, sat down and gazed out of the window without even noticing were she was heading. Her daze was interrupted when the bus driver gave a shout.

'Excuse me dear, where are you headed to?'

Looking up, Grace answered 'I'm going to Hope Street.' She had arranged the meeting at a trendy designer hotel in the city centre.

'No you're not. This is the last stop on the route!' The bus driver shook his head indignantly in response to Grace's demeanour and said 'You're on the wrong bus, pet. You should have got the 38, not the 43.'

Grace felt rage well up inside of her, suddenly becoming aware that she hadn't bothered to check the number when she got on the bus. She stood up, walked abruptly past the driver and jumped off. Standing alone outside, she tried to figure out where she was. A chilly autumn wind whipped up causing her to shiver.

'Don't worry, perhaps this is the right place for you after all?' the driver shouted, as he pulled away.

What a strange thing to say thought Grace, watching the bus disappear into the distance.

Standing on the pavement she felt foolish and immediately began to criticise herself, 'How could I be so utterly stupid? I am such an idiot.'

It was now clear that she would miss the interview. She was nowhere near the city centre let alone the trendy hotel. Feeling guilty and trying desperately to think of a plausible excuse, she looked up the number for "The Key" on her mobile.

The woman answered in an energetic and upbeat voice, and Grace could feel the positive vibe coming through the phone.

'Why do these people always sound so happy?' Grace was irritated.

'Hi, it's Grace from the PR agency. I am supposed to be meeting up with you today.'

'Hi Grace, It's great to hear from you. I am so looking forward to seeing you.'

Grace fell silent. 'I'm afraid I am not going to make it. I have taken a little detour, wrong bus!' She had already decided to tell the truth.

'Oh that's okay Grace. Call me later and we can reschedule. I am sure we will get the opportunity to meet again. Everything happens for a reason. That's how it all works.'

What did she mean by that? It reminded her of the bus driver's strange comment just a few minutes ago.

'Oh, thank you for being so understanding.' She liked the sound of her. Grace immediately felt a real sense of loss; regretting that she had blown the opportunity of meeting her that morning.

She checked out her location. She didn't know this area at all. It seemed a little run down but despite the gloom, she could sense an energy of some kind. She had a sudden picture of this desolate little place being a hub of activity and the heart of a vibrant community. She had a strange feeling that at any point it would magically come to life, just like in "Brigadoon", one of her favourite childhood movies. Where did that come from? Grace thought, surprised at the memory from her past randomly popping into her mind.

The moment was broken by sweet, angelic music. It was hypnotic and drew Grace in slowly. It was the purest sound that she had heard for a long time, and instantly transported her back to a small town in the Province of Perugia in Italy where she had holidayed years before. The music was coming from a nearby church. She stopped outside and looked at the building, stretching her neck way back to view the spire at the top of the once lofty Gothic structure.

Although cold and run down, Grace could still see the remnants of some interesting features including a row of impressive colonnettes and a profusion of flying buttresses. Through the layers of peeling black paint, she could also see traces of intricate and swirling circular designs carved into the two large wooden doors which guarded the entrance. One of the doors was slightly ajar and the faint notes floated out to meet her, curling into long fingers and beckoning her to enter.

Grace wasn't religious but she always liked spiritual places; it didn't matter what belief system they practiced. On holidays she often found herself visiting places of worship; Christian, Hindu, Buddhist and Muslim; whatever sacred location she stumbled upon, that was open and allowed her in. She liked to experience the peaceful serenity and the tangible energy of prayer. She also loved the feeling of connection and oneness.

The clouds overhead quickly closed in, enveloping everything in their path. The grey streets turned almost black. Huge droplets of water bounced a foot high off the pavement. Yes, she thought, obviously it was going to rain today, as I didn't bring my umbrella! Grace decided to shelter in the church for a moment to keep dry.

As the door creaked open Grace gasped at what she saw. In stark contrast to the mostly rundown facade on the outside, the interior was beautiful. Stately pillars rose to the ceiling, candles flickered, their flames casting shadows that danced against the stone walls. Statues of saints bowed their heads and looked down at her sympathetically, as if they were almost expecting her. The altar was a rich and ornate body of glowing gold and red, worthy and ready for divine adoration. The space was empty and silent save for her footsteps. She could hear her own breath and feel her heart thumping in her chest.

She sat down on a long wooden bench and lightly touched the pew in front of her. Closing her eyes she immediately sensed the years of faithful prayer. Grace breathed in deeply and felt a contented calmness wash over her. As she opened her eyes and glanced up, she was struck by a kaleidoscope of rainbow light streaming through the beautiful stained glass windows.

Her attention was drawn to two particular windows. Their colours were astonishing; Mediterranean purples, greens, deep pinks and golds. Both windows featured beautiful women. In one window the woman had her arms outstretched in front of her with an open book in her hands. In the other, the woman stood with drawings in her hand and the world at her feet. For some strange reason Grace felt an odd connection, and wondered who they were.

Time seemed to stand still in the silence. What happened to the singing? Had she imagined it? She thought about praying, but wasn't sure how to or what she should be praying for. Losing whatever faith she might have had long ago, she wasn't quite sure what she believed anymore.

Lost in thought, Grace was startled when she heard the door open and a set of high heels click-click down the aisle. A furry faux leopard-skin coat sat in a pew directly across from her. Grace's eyes were suddenly drawn to the wearer of the coat. It was an old lady.

As the woman took off the Paisley pattern brown scarf she had wrapped around her head, Grace saw her face for the first time. She could make out a warm, welcoming smile and youthful, luminous skin. The old lady smoothed down her grey hair which was scraped back with wisps falling to the side of her head. With her big dark eyes framed in quirky black-rimmed glasses, she looked like a wise old owl. There was a brightness surrounding her that seemed to light up everything and everywhere. Grace wondered if she was real or some kind of ethereal figure that only she could see. Grace watched as the woman then gently closed her eyes and started to breathe slowly. She had an odd smile on her face and looked happy for no apparent reason.

The rain finally stopped and sunlight began to pour through the windows. A golden aura illuminated the inside of the church and drifting dust particles were suddenly exposed in rays of shimmering light.

Grace felt a strange attraction to the old lady, a sort of curiosity that couldn't be explained. She didn't know why she felt drawn to her, she just did. She felt compelled to talk to her but had no idea why or what to say. Just as she found the courage to speak, the old lady stood up, gathered her things and walked past, moving in the direction of a candle stall positioned to the left of the alter. Before she knew it, Grace was standing right beside the old lady. They both picked up candles, lit them and stood side by side wrapped in the silence and deep in thought.

'Hello' the old lady said turning to look at Grace. 'I believe you would like to speak to me?'

'I would?' Grace wondered how the old lady had known this. Had she read my mind?

The old lady touched Grace's arm gently, looked at her with knowing eyes and said 'We have much to chat about. Come with me and we can talk.'

Grace felt safe and followed as the old lady click-clicked her way out of the church, stopping only to put some coins into a large wooden collection box built into the cold stone wall as they exited.

CHAPTER 2

SYNCHRONICITY

Outside, it felt like a totally new day; the previous grey and darkening skies now a brilliant blue with the sun shining bright, soaking up the rain from the shiny wet pavements.

The old lady led Grace down a cobbled alleyway at the side of the church, and along a narrow pavement, until they reached a solid wooden door in the tall stone wall which lined the lane. She pulled out a large ornate key from deep inside her coat pocket and unlocked the door.

Stepping inside, Grace was greeted by a stunning walled garden. There was an explosion of colour from a choir of exotic flowers, and the heady aroma of the tropical plants that edged the garden. She wondered why the garden was in full bloom in autumn when everything elsewhere was shutting down for a long hard winter slumber. It was all very curious.

'What is this place? It's so magical' Grace said, as she caught her breath.

'Come with me, there's more' and the old lady motioned to Grace as they navigated their way through a beautiful spiral labyrinth of miniature pink rose hedges.

They approached an elegant black wrought iron gate, its curved top framed with sprawling ivy and old English roses. As Grace peered through the gate's iron tendrils she gasped. An imposing Victorian sandstone building, encircled by a lush green lawn, and edged with French lavender, stood majestically before her.

As she moved closer to the house, Grace could see ornate embellishments and statues carved into the stone. The figure of a woman wearing a tall plumed riding hat protected the main entrance. Grace thought she was very pretty. Two women resembling mythical Greek goddesses were sculpted into the gables of the building. One had her arm rested on a small pedestal whilst holding a book in her other hand with the word "Literature" carved above. The second woman embraced an easel and had the title "Art" carved beneath her delicate feet. Grace realised immediately that they were the same figures that she had seen on the stained glass windows in the church.

But it was the roof of the building that took her breath away. It was constructed of gold and silver stained glass depicting an assemblage of world-famous inventors, philosophers, writers, poets and artists. She had never seen anything like it before.

The old lady took Grace's hand and led her across a little patio at the side of the house. Entering through two large French doors they stepped into a delightful morning room. A welcoming fire crackled in the hearth, and the delicious smell of burning wood filled Grace's nose.

'Do you live here? It's truly amazing.'

'Yes, I do. Although I prefer to think of myself more as the custodian, Grace. That way I know I will never take any of this for granted.' And with that the old lady scanned the room with a satisfied smile. 'I believe that life gifts us with things to take care of for a while and these gifts also include many of the people in our lives.'

Grace noticed how slight the old lady was, but she wasn't frail. Instead, she seemed strong and somehow full of life and purpose. She also noticed that the old lady already knew her name. How strange she thought.

The old lady ushered Grace towards two brown leather armchairs and invited her to sit. Grace had never felt comfort like it; it was as if the chair was moulding itself around her. The old lady busied herself making tea and was soon pouring from a dainty silver teapot into two mismatched china tea cups with bold floral patterns printed on them. Hot steam, with the sweetest smell, spiraled upwards and tickled Grace's nostrils as it rose. The hot delicate liquid softened her mouth and seemed to give her an instant inner glow.

The two women sat closely together and chatted intimately. It was quite unusual for Grace to talk about herself so openly, especially with someone she didn't know. And when she did have in-depth conversations like this, it was as a journalist and she controlled the dialogue.

To her complete surprise, the role was now reversed. She found herself answering questions and telling the old lady about her life and her job with a PR agency in the city. She disclosed that although she was well paid for what she did, she was weighed down by the deadlines and working into the early hours of the morning. When Grace had tried to re–balance her workload and leave the office a little earlier in the evening, she was defeated by guilt and the fear of how she might be perceived. This meant that she worked much later than she needed to, or was effective for her to do so. She suspected that most of the team did the same for the sake of keeping up appearances, and also to fulfil the unwritten part of their corporate job spec.

Grace disliked the competitive atmosphere in the office. She and her colleagues constantly jockeyed for position and vied to produce the best articles and news items to win the favour of their egotistical boss. This approach created a very tangible and negative vibe amongst all of them and certainly didn't bode well for camaraderie or social bonding. She did not enjoy working in this way and it was definitely affecting her mood and behaviour. It was sapping her energy.

And then there was "the longing." Grace had no idea where this feeling came from, why it was there, or what it was for. But it had gnawed and gnawed away at her for years. She had such a strong sense that she was supposed to be somewhere else doing something else. She did have a half-baked notion of writing a book, but this had long since been discarded and left on an imaginary bookshelf in her head. Grace lacked the confidence or courage to make any sort of major change in her life. And as far as writing a book was concerned, she didn't believe that she had anything important to say or that someone would want to read her book anyway!

Grace caught herself. Why am I telling her all of this? Thinking that she had already said way too much, she stopped talking abruptly. But for the first time, Grace had heard herself articulate just how empty her life had become and how unhappy she was with it. She had somehow lost herself, and it felt like self betrayal. She began to fidget in her seat uncomfortably.

The old lady sensed the change in Grace's mood and intuitively switched the topic of conversation. 'Do you believe in synchronicity, Grace?' she asked.

Grace hesitated. 'Like luck or coincidence? Is that what you mean?'

The old lady replied by asking 'Why do you think you are here with me right now? Think about your day, Grace. Was it your intention to come here when you set off this morning?'

Grace looked up and thought hard. She really didn't know how she had ended up in this chair, in this fabulous room, sitting across from an old lady she had only just met. It really had been the most bizarre day ever. Grace recounted the day in her mind.

'No, it was definitely not in my plan to come here, in fact I shouldn't be here at all. Oversleeping, car breaking down, wrong bus, missed appointment, everything about today was just wrong.' However, something was telling Grace that maybe it wasn't so wrong after all. It was right. She was exactly where she was meant to be, somehow. She suddenly remembered the odd comment that the bus driver had made earlier that morning.

The old lady smiled and said, 'You'll find that events and people come into your life for a reason, Grace. We don't always know why, immediately. It can take a while for it to become clear. Often it's only through joining the dots and upon reflection, that the answers are revealed. The important thing is to recognise that nothing ever happens by accident. Everything happens for a reason. Often we ignore the signs and pass them off as coincidences. Most people are "asleep" and don't make the connections. But sooner or later life will present a series of "synchronistic" events that conspire, like today, and force us to sit up and take notice.'

'Why did you come into the church today?'

Grace laughed a little, 'Because it started to rain.'

But that wasn't the real story and Grace knew it. Something else had made her stop outside the church and it wasn't just the music and the singing.

The old lady continued, 'Sometimes when life stops you in your tracks, you become present, and become much more aware of what is actually going on around you. You notice things that you might never have otherwise noticed before. Appearances can be deceptive too. Nothing is ever quite as it seems. What did you think of the church today before you came in?'

Grace admitted, 'I thought it was pretty run down, broken and crumbling. Normally I would have just walked on by.'

'Exactly' the old lady said. 'And the same with my beautiful garden hiding behind that dismal alleyway out there! Grace, we have to learn to look below the surface to see the riches that lie beneath.'

Grace considered all of this carefully. Yes, looking at the start to her day, everything had gone wrong. But sitting here with the old lady in this spectacular building with its enchanting secret garden, she felt like she had been given some kind of gift, an opportunity, a little piece of magic. She felt incredibly inspired. It was an unfamiliar feeling for Grace to experience and she liked it.

She thought about the singing and asked the old lady, 'Do you sing?'

Suddenly the old lady let out quite a belly laugh which caught Grace completely by surprise. It seemed to stop time and shake the walls. Grace couldn't help but laugh too. It was infectious and it felt good to let herself go for once and join in.

The old lady took a breath and said, 'Well, I have been known to do a great "Barbra Streisand" at a party.'

Grace laughed at the picture that conjured up in her mind but didn't quite know what to make of it. She got the feeling that nothing about this old lady should surprise her.

The old lady glanced at her watch and broke the silence by saying 'It's time for you to go, my dear.'

It then dawned on Grace that she would soon be back in the real world and she felt a curious resistance to that thought.

She wondered what would happen next. She didn't want this to be the last time they would meet. Intuitively though, she knew she would see her again. Grace was supposed to be here; there was a reason behind all of this, although she wasn't quite sure why…. yet. But she was sure that it was the start of something positive, a journey, an adventure and that thought made her excited.

The old lady then said, 'I want you to do something for me.' Grace nodded. 'Meet me here this Saturday at 10am. Can you do that?'

Without any hesitation Grace said 'Of course I will. That would be lovely.'

She smiled as she buttoned up her coat. She paused for a moment and looked all around the room, taking in the whole experience and storing it in her memory. She looked at the old lady and said 'Thank you so much for the wonderful tea.'

Grace stepped out of the house and pulled her scarf tight around her neck. There was a chill in the air and the garden was held in a hushed silence. She felt as though the trees and plants were watching her. She could see the tall buildings beyond the wooden gate reminding her of the world outside, a world that she had momentarily forgotten. She unlatched the gate and walked out into the alleyway, stepping on an empty *Irn Bru* can as she began her journey home.

CHAPTER 3

CURIOSITY

Unusually, Grace found herself waking up just before her alarm went off. She was even getting out of bed with a spring in her step. She couldn't quite put her finger on exactly why, but she felt better for it. Colleagues at the office had noticed and commented about her energy and chattiness. Very surprisingly, it was rubbing off on them too!

Despite all of this however, she was still struggling to get to grips with the strange events from earlier that week. She had no idea of the meaning behind her "synchronistic" meeting with the old lady, but one thing was for sure, she believed there was a reason and knew that it would reveal itself soon enough.

It was now Saturday and she remembered her promise to meet the old lady. She was looking forward to it. For some reason she thought of the bus driver as she picked up her car keys. There was something about him. Her curiosity got the better of her and she put her car keys back on the hall table, deciding to take the bus instead.

'Hello there' said the bus driver. 'Are you getting on the wrong bus again today?' he laughed.

'Okay, okay, you win! It was the right bus after all' admitted Grace, albeit a little reluctantly.

'I know' the bus driver said with a smile.

This time Grace took a moment to pause and look at the driver as she paid her bus fare. She studied his face. His eyes were a bright beautiful bluey-green colour. His head was nearly bald but he had little grey side burns to make up for it. A long strand of hair swept all the way across the top of his head framing the character lines etched across his forehead. He had a round face, a neatly trimmed moustache and big jolly red cheeks. He would have been really handsome in his youth thought Grace, and she smiled as she sat down.

Grace relaxed into her seat, resting her head against the steamed up window. She let her thoughts drift off and gradually came back to the present when she realised that the bus had stopped. That's strange. I am the only person on this bus again, and I can't remember it making any stops.

'That's you here' said the driver.

As she passed him to disembark he said, 'Do you read much?'

Grace was bewildered by the question. 'No, not really. Not nowadays. I used to read a lot though.'

'I love books. I borrow them from my local library. You can get any book you want there, it's quite amazing and best of all they're free. Just as well because I can read two to three in a week!' the bus driver boasted.

As she stepped off the bus he cheerily shouted out that his current reading list comprised of two books; one about the history of New York City and the other documenting the rise and fall of the Roman Empire.

'Eh, that's great, thanks for that' Grace said, surprised by the randomness of the conversation.

Grace didn't know it at the time, but over the coming months, she would grow very fond of the bus driver and his positive upbeat way of being. She would also become very interested in the books he was reading and find a heartfelt appreciation for his vast knowledge and the fact that he was kindly sharing it with her. He was a storyteller. She would learn so much about the world, past, present and future, through the stories he would share with her during their short bus journeys together.

Grace felt light and happy as she walked from the bus. She felt like skipping but stopped herself by thinking of how silly she would look. She saw the church and could hear the faint sound of singing again. It was a hymn she recognised from her childhood and she smiled at the happy memory.

She wasn't visiting the church today and instead turned directly into the hidden lane. Little bits of debris whirled around the cobbled stones and danced at her feet.

As she approached the entrance to the garden, her hair blew across her face, restricting her sight temporarily and causing her to trip. Banging her head against the solid oak wood door she quickly tried to right herself. 'Ouch' she exclaimed, rubbing her head.

How am I going to get in? I don't have a key. There was no doorbell and no one could hear her. The old lady's house was a good way into the garden. Of course she didn't think to ask the old lady for a mobile phone number; she wondered if she would even have a phone. She stood and pondered for a few minutes rubbing her head, which had the start of a small bump. Just then the door slowly started to creak open.

Grace couldn't see anyone as she stepped inside. Tentatively she began to look around. She felt like an explorer in a strange new world. Plants, flowers, bushes, trees, lush green lawn; yes, it was all there, it was real. She noticed a chunky robin who was watching her with his little beady eyes. He hopped about on the lower branch of an old oak tree as he proudly puffed out his huge red feathery chest.

Everything was completely silent and peaceful. It was then that she noticed the fragrant tropical plants and flowers again and the same question surfaced. Why is this garden so lush and flourishing in autumn?

As she entered through the ornamental gates at the end of the walled garden she noticed the lights were on in the old lady's morning room. The patio doors opened to reveal the old lady standing with her arms outstretched ready to embrace Grace with a big, warm, heartfelt hug.

'There you are. Come in dear. Perfect timing. I've got some tea ready for you.'

Grace followed the old lady into the house. The leather armchairs were set out side by side in front of the fire that glowed in the hearth. Flames gently flickered, sparkled and crackled.

Just as she was about to sit down, Grace noticed lots of photographs featuring the old lady dotted around the room. They beckoned her to investigate. Perhaps she might find something out about this mysterious little woman. The old lady followed her gaze. 'Have a look if you want' she invited.

Grace moved round the room picking the photo frames up one by one. She had always been fascinated by other people's photos. She loved seeing their special moments captured and sealed forever. They told stories. Stories of the wonderful diversity of life, capturing the spectrum of human emotion; happiness and joy and even sadness and pain. Stewards of precious memories.

There was an abundance of photographs depicting several generations of family at seasonal and social gatherings; eating, talking, laughing, dancing and singing. An invisible thread of love connecting everyone. Grace noticed one particular photo with the old lady looking very glamorous, with a microphone held close to her lips. Grace wondered if she was singing a "Barbra Streisand" number and laughed to herself at the thought.

Many of the old lady's pictures were black and white. It was strange seeing her as a young woman. Grace recognised her straight away even though the fashion and hairstyles varied. Some of them were really quite funny. There was a great photo with the old lady in her teenage years, sitting on a Triumph motorcycle with her friends cheering in the background.

A small silver frame held a wonderful image of a petite gymnast, beaming triumphantly with a red ribbon around her neck, supporting a shiny bronze medal.

'Oh did you know I used to be a gymnast, Grace? Yes, that was until I had my little accident. And at that, the old lady lifted her shirt sleeve to reveal a rather nasty looking scar on her left arm. 'Doesn't stop me from doing the odd cartwheel however!' and she laughed heartily.

There was a lovely photo of the old lady cuddling a little black and white furry dog, and another with a pretty young girl and a white boxer dog which had one tan-brown ear and big slobbery jaws. Grace smiled. The two women looked almost like sisters. 'That's my daughter' the old lady said and gave Grace a beautiful smile full of pride. Grace suddenly experienced an unfamiliar, but very pleasant, sensation move through her heart.

The old lady's photos all seemed to capture her looking happy and spirited with lots of vibrant people and exciting things going on. Images of celebrations. One in particular caught Grace's attention. It was a group of confident women living it up in New York, weighed down with shopping bags from famous stores, whilst the old lady waved a bottle of pink champagne in the air above her head. Beside this stood a series of professional looking photos with the old lady on a podium addressing a large and diverse audience; people of every age, background and nationality, listening intently. The tiny figure of a woman stood centre stage with the lights creating a magical silver aura around her.

Grace knew she was holding mementos of a treasured and purposeful life in her hand.

Feeling tired, Grace sighed. She was suddenly caught up in a torrent of thoughts and images of her own past. Grace didn't have a lot of personal photographs. She had a few with her mother; some on holiday and at birthdays. She didn't have a big family or a large group of friends. She kept herself pretty much to herself. And anyway, she was self-conscious and never liked seeing herself in photos. Even when she was told how pretty she looked, she never believed it; choosing instead to always find a fault, whether it be with her face, her hair or her shape.

She had one photo on display. It was taken on her first day of school, by a neighbour, outside her front door. Grace wore her blonde hair in pigtails, crowned with a blue striped hair-band, a crisp school uniform and a brown leather satchel which hung diagonally across her new school blazer. She was smiling from ear to ear in it. She was happy then. Her mother and father stood proudly behind her tiny outline. It was the only one she had of the three of them together. Her eyes filled at that thought and she choked back tears, quickly dismissing her emotions. Her head started to hurt and she convinced herself that it was the bump.

Suddenly she became aware of the old lady studying her. She sat down and picked up her cup, hiding her face behind it.

'How did you feel after our "synchronistic" meeting on Monday, Grace?' the old lady asked peering over her black-framed glasses.

Grace thought for a moment. 'To be honest, it was as if I had dreamt or imagined it all. Maybe I wanted to be sure that it had actually happened. That's why I decided to come back. I was curious.'

The old lady smiled. 'Perfect, Grace. Curiosity is the perfect place to start any journey.'

The old lady then surprised her by asking 'Do you know what Leonardo da Vinci is famous for?'

'Of course' Grace answered, 'The Mona Lisa.'

'Yes Grace, that's true, but what most people don't know, is that Leonardo was also a talented sculptor, architect, musician, scientist, mathematician, engineer, inventor, anatomist, geologist, writer and botanist…phew!'

'Really? He was all of those things?' asked Grace 'That's unbelievable. How on earth did he manage to cram all of that into one lifetime?'

'That's an interesting question, Grace. The answer lies in "potential." Leonardo tapped into, and unlocked his potential. We all have this very same opportunity; to dream, to dare, to learn and to be. We do not need to be defined by age or limited by only one idea of ourselves.'

'But tell me, where do think this potential and his creative genius started?' Without giving Grace any time to answer, the old lady leapt out of her seat, threw her hands in the air dramatically and announced in a broken Italian accent …'Curiosità!'

'Grace. It all began with "Curiosità!" and if you speak Italian, you will know that means… *to approach life with unquenchable curiosity and an insatiable quest for learning.'*

She then finished with a little curtsy saying 'Grazie!' in the same broken accent, before bursting into hysterical laughter.

Grace was startled by her outburst and energy.

'That's how everyone should approach life, Grace. Keep our minds open. Be more childlike, playful and fascinated about life. That way, everything becomes easier to learn.'

'Look at me; I'm still learning something new every single day. I am open to all of life's possibilities. I believe anything can happen, even at my age! When we think like this Grace, life becomes creative and presents us with all sorts of exciting opportunities. We can either grab them with both hands… or not, but in order to even see them in the first place, we need to be open and curious.'

'You are already using those principles. You made the choice to come here today. You were curious, and opened yourself up to an exciting new possibility' and with that the old lady began to clap her hands excitedly.

Grace smiled. She felt very pleased with herself. 'Thank you, or should I say "Grazie"?' she giggled.

'It's funny you should mention this, because I have been feeling excited all week. I have had so much energy but I didn't know why. This all makes sense now.' In that exact moment Grace connected her new lease of life and increased energy with curiosity.

'Now you have another choice to make' said the old lady. 'You can continue with me on a magical life adventure or you can choose to stop right here. What will you choose?'

'You mean an adventure starting right now, today?' Grace was confused.

'Yes, right now. In this powerful, present, moment of now.' And with that the old lady opened her arms toward Grace inviting her to begin.

Grace was silent for a few minutes, she felt a knot in her stomach as fear kicked in. 'Go where... for what?' She had so many questions she would normally have wanted answered first.

But instead she quietly said 'Yes.' It was completely out of character but the word just seemed to pop out of her mouth before she could stop it. She then repeated 'Yes, I will go with you' in an energetic and assertive tone just to convince herself that little bit more.

The old lady jumped up and applauded again. 'Molto Bene!, Grace. I thought you'd say that. Congratulations! That's the correct answer' and she laughed this time even louder than before. Clearly excited, she then did a funny little dance around the room before falling back into her chair in a fit of giggles.

CHAPTER 4

CREATION

Are you ready?' The old lady beckoned to Grace as if they were going to head off somewhere, but instead relaxed into her seat, took a deep breath and closed her eyes.

Grace watched her, but wasn't exactly sure what was happening, or what she was supposed to do.

As if sensing how she was feeling, the old lady said 'Grace, sit back and just breathe, breathe deeply. Allow your mind to be still. That will calm you.'

Grace did as she was instructed and began to focus on her breathing. Sinking further and further into the soft leather chair, she felt the sides begin to wrap around her like huge bear-hug arms. She felt safe and secure, and soon found herself drifting and dozing, before falling into a deep relaxed state.

Grace slipped into a sleepy daydream. She could hear the old lady talking in the background, 'Clear your mind, be still and let go of all thoughts. Open your mind, Grace, and let's see where it leads you.'

Grace woke feeling a cold wind shiver through her body. She turned to the old lady and said, 'I'm so sorry; I think I must have fallen asleep. I had the strangest dream; I dreamt I was at the seaside. I could actually smell the salty sharpness of the sea air and hear the seagulls', Grace said disbelievingly.

The old lady smiled and took Grace's hand. 'Come on, I want to show you something' and she led Grace to the door. When she opened it, instead of the patio and the lush green lawn, they stepped out into a vast never-ending carpet of white sand.

Grace blinked and blinked again, blinded by the light. She let out a gasp. 'How could this be? Where had the garden gone?' Everything she expected to see outside had disappeared.

Grace fell to her knees, picked up a handful of sand, and watched it slowly trickle through her fingers. It tickled her. She looked up and could see waves gently rippling in the distance. It was hypnotic. The sun's rays glistened and bounced off the electric blue ocean and the bright white expanse around her. It was how she imagined the beginning of the world to look and feel.

'Follow me' said the old lady and she led Grace across the sand to two red deckchairs. Grace and the old lady sat down together and gazed out across the perfect horizon.

'Am I dreaming? I haven't actually woken up yet, have I?' Grace said as she turned to the old lady, who was sitting casually beside her, as if this type of thing happened every day.

The old lady laughed, and as she did so the sound of her laughter was carried off in the wind and out to sea.

She suddenly became very serious. 'Grace, I want to talk to you about Creation.'

The old lady continued. 'Let's start with the most wonderful of all creations, children. Children have extremely vivid imaginations. Their minds are alive, alert, and awake. No idea is too big for them. At an early age their thoughts have no judgment of size or possibility. They are truly natural little creators. Children are like little blank sheets of paper, waiting for their very own magical stories to be written, music scores to dance to and award winning movie scripts to star in.'

The old lady paused, looking up with a huge grin as if she was creating this idea in her head right there and then.

'Children have an inherent ability to create. They are curious and are always asking why; *Why is it like that? Why does that happen? But why?* They instinctively know what is right for them and they have a very clear sense of what they need or want at every stage. If allowed, they will busy themselves with learning how to achieve it.' The old lady was speaking as if she was a child herself.

'But then adults come along. They think that just because they are bigger and older, that they are somehow smarter and know better. And soon the life-long process begins. Children's creative space is hijacked and those beautiful little minds are filled with adult views, and limiting perceptions of the world.'

Grace thought back to her childhood, and particularly to school. Whenever she would ask *why?,* she was always told *...just because,* or *that's just the way it is Grace.*

She remembered how she used to let her imagination go wild with plans about doing amazing things and becoming like the people she admired. But whenever she shared her thoughts and dreams, she was always told 'It isn't good to have grandiose ideas. It's better to keep your imagination in check. Keep things realistic.' Because of this, Grace believed that there was no point in dreaming or building up expectations, and that it was wrong to do so.

'Who told you that?' the old lady snapped. She seemed really angry. 'That's exactly the kind of thinking that ensures you'll never create your heart's desire.'

She looked at Grace pitifully. 'When you believe that your dreams are silly and impossible, or that you will never be able to achieve them, then of course, that's exactly what will happen. No surprises there!'

The old lady looked sad as she spoke, as if she was experiencing pain. 'And so Grace, you can see how our natural creativity is stifled at a very young age and we lose touch with our creative power. But it doesn't need to be that way.'

The old lady then began to tell Grace a story from her own childhood.

'I was aware at a very early age that things I dreamt about would often appear within my reality, as if by magic. It was as if I was creating them from out of nowhere.'

'I remember wanting a deckchair, exactly like the one you are sitting on right now.' The old lady laughed.

Grace looked at the deckchairs. 'What an odd thing for a young girl to want' and she smiled thinking nothing should surprise her about this bizarre old lady.

The old lady relaxed back into the chair. She put her arms behind her head and looked right up to the glorious blue sky and began to explain. 'I remember as a teenager, deckchairs became all the rage. A real trend. I really wanted one but I had no money to buy it.'

'I know it seems crazy but I used to think about this deckchair all the time and imagine it in my bedroom beside my bookshelves. I imagined a red one with white stripes. In my imagination I would sit on it. I could quite literally feel myself relaxing into it whilst reading my books. I loved the idea of having one and would cut pictures out and put them on my dream board beside my bed. It made me happy when I looked at my red and white imaginary deckchair.'

The old lady's smile widened. 'One weekend I decided to go to a local jumble sale. I used to love going to jumble sales. I would spend hours meandering through, dusty scout halls; wandering aimlessly through rows of rickety wooden chairs and tables. I would pick up old framed pictures of the countryside and farms. They always reminded me of summer holidays in Ireland, shared with my sister, cousin and gran.'

'I would smile at myself as I caught my reflection in the large gilded mirrors that sat grandly behind the dainty floral china tea sets and silver plated teapots.

'Jumble sales were full of magical old things and oh how I loved the discarded treasures. Thousand-piece jigsaws of our amazing world depicting wild animals to be discovered on a safari. And board games - Monopoly with houses on Mayfair; Snakes and Ladders or Cluedo; murders in the kitchen or the library by Mrs. White!

'I loved to look through the rows of second-hand books on the old wooden bookshelves that lined the halls. I was always on the hunt for collections of "The Famous Five" and "The Secret Seven." I found my first "Narnia" books by C.S. Lewis at a jumble sale.'

'To me a jumble sale was an Aladdin's cave of sparkling costume jewellery, exotic vintage dresses, t-bar high heeled shoes, purple feather boas and old leopard-skin coats. I loved them and still do.'

Grace noticed a delicate little tear in the old lady's eye as she remembered it all so vividly.

Suddenly, the old lady sat up straight and said, 'One Saturday, I was stopped right in my tracks. There it was. A brand new red and white deckchair. Exactly like the one I had been picturing in my mind. I was astonished. I couldn't believe my eyes.'

'How much is that deckchair?' I asked the man at the stall. When he told me how much it was, I realised I had the exact amount of money in my little velvet purse. I was so excited I nearly jumped up and kissed him.

'Yes I will have it, please' I screamed with excitement as I handed over my coin. I took my deckchair from the stand and hugged it to my heart. I skipped and danced with it under my arm all the way home. You have no idea how happy I felt.'

Grace was totally engrossed in this story. She had always loved stories and this was a particularly good one.

'But something else happened in that moment, Grace. Something so much more important. I saw the link between my thoughts and the deckchair magically appearing. I knew that I had influenced this outcome in some way. I just wasn't sure how.'

'Now luckily for me, I had an inquisitive and curious mind. It's a trait to be found in most scientists. Did I mention I was a scientist, Grace?' and the old lady just continued talking without giving Grace the opportunity to reply.

'Anyway, I decided to retrace my steps and think about the process that I had used to get my deckchair. I discovered I had used a very deliberate process; that there is indeed a "**Creation Process**" with very definite steps.'

'The first step was to think about something that I wanted to have and picture it in my mind. In my case, the deckchair. The second step was to talk to myself and create pictures and stories about it. This then produced the feeling of having it, and so the third step took place. Because I felt it, I believed it was possible and as a result I saw it. It became a reality.'

'Now that's what I call an important discovery!' and the old lady afforded herself a round of applause.

'Does it all make sense to you, Grace?' the old lady asked.

Grace's cogs were turning; she was struggling to process everything. 'Okay, that's a great story but is it really that simple? You are telling me that you just need to see something you want in your imagination, believe you can have it and you will get it?' Grace was sceptical. She recalled how she had often wished for things, but unlike this story, she was always disappointed when they had never shown up.

'Ah, Grace. That's the mistake most people make. They think seeing is believing' the old lady mocked. 'But it's actually the other way around. You have to **Believe** it first, and then you will you see it!'

'Grace, wishing is just the first step in the process, I am talking about **Creation.**'

CHAPTER 5

IN THE BEGINNING

H ere is what I know for sure.' The old lady seemed to grow in size as she spoke.

'There is a power that can reveal hidden veins of riches and uncover treasures that we can only dream of, Grace. There is a force that we can call on for a fulfilled and happy life of abundance. Our great saints and the sages of India knew of it; great leaders have known of it too, as have many of the people who have achieved remarkable things in the world. They have all demonstrated the efficacy of this true principle. And Grace, it can work for you too!'

The old lady continued. 'Your success in life does not altogether depend on your ability or skills. More often it depends on your ability to grasp opportunities presented to you, including the knowledge of this creative power that I am sharing with you now.'

'Opportunities in life come by Creation, not by chance. Nothing happens by accident. Everything is connected. You yourself, either now or in the past, have created the opportunities in your life. But, like most people, you may not be aware of it.'

'Creation is not a new concept. It goes way back to the beginning of time. Did you know that in the ancient Aramaic language the word Abracadabra means "I will create as I speak?" she asked rhetorically. 'I'm not telling you anything new, Grace. There are literally hundreds of references to this idea in the world's great holy and scientific books. All things are created out of nothing. *No-thing.*'

'For, whatever we think and feel, the creative spirit of life is bound to faithfully manifest and so does Creation begin.'

Grace sat on her deckchair, listening. 'Okay, I was willing to run with the deckchair story, but the idea that we can create? You talk about Creation and it sounds so natural. When I think about Creation, I think of God creating the world.'

'I think about immense and extraordinary creations. I think of the truly great artists, writers, architects, inventors; people who have created incredible things in their life time. It's only gifted people who can create. Not ordinary people like me!' Grace was feeling very uncomfortable with all of this.

'Yes Grace, I can understand why you might believe that story but there is something else. It is said that we have been made in the image of *The Creator.*'

The old lady paused for a few minutes and stared at her intently before posing the next question.

'If that is true, is it possible then, that we can also create?'

The old lady raised an eyebrow and looked at Grace in the most provocative way.

'This has gone too far', Grace exclaimed.

'Grace, listen to me. We are all Creators. We are powerful creative beings. Every single one of us. And I am not just talking about being able to draw or paint! We are capable of creating our world.' The old lady paused to allow this idea to sink in. She then continued 'But sadly, like you, most people are unaware of this possibility or they just resist the idea completely.'

'Everything you are or have in your life just now - you created it on some level. I may have used the simple story of my deckchair but **"The Creation Process"** applies to everything. The Creation Process just is. It is not new. It's as old as time itself and bound up in ancient philosophies, universal laws and science.'

'You have to let go of your old fashioned thinking, Grace' the old lady said lovingly.

She then finished by saying 'You, yes you, are capable of creating great things. Anyone can create amazing things, Grace. This is not just for the realms of the so-called genius. We can all access this creative power. It is within us all.'

CHAPTER 6

DREAMS

All week Grace had been agitated and restless. Feeling very uneasy about the previous week's revelations. She found herself constantly writing random thoughts in her notebook. It helped exorcise the concerns she had about everything the old lady had told her. It was preposterous for her to think of herself as a Creator. How could she entertain such a thought?

Her mood was not helped by the fact that she was waking up in the middle of the night sweating, with energy tingling throughout her body. She couldn't sleep because of it. It felt as if someone had turned on an electrical switch inside her and now she couldn't turn it off. The odd snatches of sleep she did get were interrupted by a recurring dream which terrified her.

It was the same dream night after night.

She was sinking helplessly into the sand. An invisible force pulled her feet from below. The sun was beating down on her face as she was sucked further and further into the quicksand. She screamed for help but no one could hear her plea. A lone seagull circled overhead. Closer and closer it came, its squawking call echoing with mocking laughter. She waved her hands frantically as her arms flailed in the air. She choked as the dry sharp sand began to fill her mouth and nostrils. She could utter no words. She could say "no–thing." She was without voice or words. As the horror of the situation registered with her she closed her eyes, now filled with salty tears. She had resigned herself to whatever fate the quicksand had in store for her. Her last thoughts were a wish for something different.

Then, she would awaken, gasping for air and exhausted.

Grace was relieved that it was Saturday again. She was keen to speak to the old lady about her thoughts on this "Creation matter" and about how she was feeling about it all. She wanted to be reassured and her questions answered.

As she was leaving, she spotted a postcard on her study desk. It was the *Salvator Mundi,* a painting by Leonardo da Vinci. She remembered picking the card up at an exhibition in London. Grace had found herself hypnotised by it for some strange reason. She had always felt an attraction to Leonardo, his genius and his works.

Now this is what I call Creation. He is a creator she thought defiantly, and decided she would give the card to the old lady to prove a point.

As she turned the postcard over she read a quote by Leonardo which was printed on the reverse:

'There are three classes of people: those who see, those who see when they are shown, those who do not see.'

'What does this mean? And why did he write that?' Grace was curious.

Before Grace knew it, she was sitting on the bus and lost in thought all over again.

'Hey, Miss. You were miles away' the driver said as he brought her back to the present.

'Yes, sorry, you're right. Are we there yet?' Grace asked.

'Yes we are. How time flies when you're daydreaming. We don't always give enough time for that if you ask me. Sometimes the best creative ideas surface when we are dreaming' he said, giving her a huge smile.

Recalling her nightmares, Grace snapped 'I am afraid I have been dreaming way too much recently!' and with that she jumped down from the bus, without saying goodbye or even giving the driver a second glance or a wave.

She walked quickly past the church and entered the lane. It was empty apart from a black cat which passed in front of her just as she approached the huge wooden door in the stone wall.

The door was unlocked and she stepped inside and into the garden. It was eerily quiet and nothing moved. For the first time it felt like a cold autumn day, it was as if the garden was reacting to her feelings. Grace shivered as though unseen eyes watched her every step. She looked up and noticed the old lady standing at the French doors.

'Good morning Grace. Come in, please take a seat' the old lady said, ushering her in and over to their usual comfy chairs.

Despite feeling anxious, Grace tried to relax and sank into her chair. The tea was already brewing in the teapot and the old lady poured.

'How have you been, Grace?' the old lady enquired.

'I brought you something' Grace said quickly to change the subject. She had no desire to open up the debate about Creation yet. 'I thought you might like it.' And she handed over the postcard.

The old lady looked at it, smiled and said 'Thank you, Grace. This is perfect. Relevant to both our beach adventure and our chats about Creation.'

Grace said nothing, waiting for the right opportunity to voice her thoughts.

Intuitively, sensing that Grace had something to say, the old lady said 'So Grace, tell me, how do you feel knowing that you are a powerful Creator?'

Grace sat upright in the chair. She was clenching her teeth, something she always did when she felt anxious and had something on her mind. She suddenly became aware that she was gripping the arms of the chair very tightly and digging her nails into the soft leather.

CHAPTER 7

I AM A CREATOR

Grace began to speak, but before she could get the words out, she found herself caught in a gripping spiral of emotion. It was terrifying. She felt as if she was back in her bad dream, being pulled downward into quicksand.

She screamed loudly as she was temporarily blinded by a glaring white light. She was falling into an abyss, her arms flailed in the air and a strong wind whipped her hair around her face. Then suddenly everything stopped.

Grace opened her eyes. She was frightened and gasped for breath. She quickly looked around to see where she was. Grace relaxed a little when she saw the old lady was next to her.

They were standing in the attic of an old house.

'Where are we? What happened to me? Did I faint?' Grace whispered. She was still shaking.

It was then that she noticed a small boy in the corner of the attic.

'There are some people I thought you should meet' the old lady said as she directed her gaze towards the boy. 'Don't worry, he can't see you. Just watch him.'

Grace looked around the room. It was scattered with all sorts of objects. Piles and piles of books had been randomly abandoned and lots of drawings lay corner to corner. Grace also noticed drawings stuck to every wall. They appeared to have been drawn by a child although a lot of thought and detail had clearly gone into them; etchings of strange animals in a magical fantasy land.

The boy was sitting at an old fashioned wooden school desk with an ink pot on the top. He was writing. Suddenly, the boy stood up. Grace jumped back, not knowing what to do. He obviously didn't know she was there and walked past her to the back of the attic, to an old standing wardrobe. He stood in front of it for a while, touched the dark wood, opened the door, stepped inside and disappeared.

'What's he doing?' whispered Grace. 'Is he hiding from someone?'

The room fell strangely silent. A soft wind began to blow gently, lifting the drawings one by one off the wall. One of the drawings floated like a feather, swirling and twirling until it landed directly at Grace's feet. She picked it up. It looked distinctive and somehow familiar. She had seen it before, but couldn't remember where.

Grace studied the drawing. It was a mystical creature with horns on its head, the torso of a man and the legs of a goat. He was carrying an umbrella and a box. He was in a wood and it was snowing. Then she remembered. Spinning around to look at the old lady, she exclaimed. 'It's the faun from Narnia! I remember.'

Grace turned the drawing over to find a faint message written on the back. She read it aloud.

'*They all began with seeing pictures in my head. At first they were not a story, just pictures. The Lion all began with a picture*

of a Faun carrying an umbrella and parcels in a snowy wood.
This picture had been in my mind since I was about sixteen.
Then one day, when I was about forty, I said to myself. Let's try
to make a story about it.'

Grace looked at the old lady; her mouth wide open in
astonishment. Losing her voice in shock she whispered 'The
little boy is C.S. Lewis!'

But before she had a chance to hear a response, a huge gust of
wind blew past her. Grace felt someone take her hand and pull
her through the air. She felt as though she was speeding through
space and time, propelled into a dark tunnel with
flashing streaks of light. Something was whizzing past her head.
It looked like figures and numbers.

Everything stopped still and Grace discovered that she was now
in an office. It was a nondescript place and deadly quiet. There
was a man standing at a window, staring outside. He was deep
in thought as though he was looking for inspiration or an escape
route from what looked like a boring and mundane day-to-day
existence.

Grace wondered where she was. Aware that the old lady was
standing beside her she felt reassured. 'Where are we now?' she
whispered curiously.

The old lady smiled. 'We're in Switzerland, the Swiss Patent
Office to be precise.'

'Why are we here?' Grace looked at the old lady, and then
quickly focused her attention back on the man. He didn't seem
to be doing much, thought Grace, as she continued to watch him
stare through the window. There was a sense of waiting.

Glancing around the office, Grace noticed symbols beginning to
appear as if by magic on the walls, in the air and everywhere

around her. Figures, letters, algebraic signs in all sizes, colours and fonts, flitting here and there. It was spellbinding, dizzying even. The vast soup eventually settled and Grace realised that she was looking at an assortment of mathematical equations. They looked like a foreign language to her.

Then, tantalizingly, five characters slowly appeared. A formula she recognised immediately. *"$E=mc^2$."*

'It's Einstein?!' she cried out as she suddenly recognised his magnificent, wild, unruly hair and disheveled, unkempt look.

'This is madness!' Grace said, looking at the old lady with wide eyes.

The old lady then told her, that it was here in the patent office that Einstein had made his most shocking and amazing discoveries.

Grace was stunned and now appreciated that he wasn't bored or just looking aimlessly out of the window after all. He was tapping into creative space, accessing the place where his groundbreaking and life-changing theories were created.

She felt so privileged to be there in that moment.

Beams of light and strings of mathematics were now dancing all around her. It was so beautiful, it made her want to cry. An inscription in Einstein's hand writing miraculously began to write itself in the air…

"Imagination is more important than knowledge… imagination encircles the world."

The lights went out and unexpectedly Grace was plunged back into darkness. A deathly silence enveloped her and she shivered.

She noticed the old lady beside her holding a lamp and she saw some faint lights flickering up ahead. Grace coughed and the sharp sound ricocheted off cold walls and returned back to her. It was as if the stone had a secret voice. The air felt heavy, musty and dead. She somehow knew that they were standing in a church crypt. She saw a monument dedicated to someone of great importance but couldn't make out who it was.

Linking arms, they started to slowly walk to the end of the narrow passageway. Stepping out into glaring sunlight, Grace squinted and held her hand up to shade her eyes.

They were in a park, but a park like no other. It was full of bright colours and odd shaped objects. There was a maze of staircases and passageways every which way she looked, built in undulating waves which made them look as though they were flowing. Dragons, snakes and lizards made of tiny brightly-coloured mosaic tiles glinted in the warm sunshine. There were tall columns and pillars, and a building that reminded Grace of the gingerbread house in the fairytale Hansel and Gretel.

Grace could see a young boy sitting cross-legged on a large flat ammonite fossil stone near the entrance to the house. He was studying mushrooms, insects, plants, pebbles and shells, so much so that he seemed to be a part of them. He was completely at one with his natural surroundings.

'Who's that?' said Grace.

'It's Antoni Gaudi, the Catalan architect' the old lady said. 'As a young boy, rheumatic problems caused him to stay at home, so he spent much of his time exploring and observing nature. His fascination with the "micro" world became the catalyst which sparked his imagination and would ultimately inspire his organic architectural works. He created from life.'

The old lady took her hand 'Come on, follow me.' They turned and walked back the way they had come and eventually they arrived at the passageway. Only now, they were no longer standing in a crypt, but inside a breathtaking church. It was clearly unfinished but still a grand architectural jewel.

Sunlight streamed down from the sky and forced its way through the patterned stonework of its massive columns which tapered off like finely pointed pencils with slightly bulbous ends.

'Do you know this place?' said the old lady.

'Yes, I've been here before' said Grace. 'It's the Sagrada Família – Gaudi's greatest unfinished work. Gaudi was buried in the crypt underneath wasn't he? That's where we were first?'

'Yes, you're right' the old lady said. 'Gaudi created many astonishing things but dedicated the last years of his life to creating this awesome masterpiece.' She continued, 'He had an incredible vision and this was his final creation. Like so many famous Creators, his vision left a huge imprint on the world.'

Grace could see the brilliance of this.

The old lady explained. 'The key to his creativity, was that he stayed absolutely true to what he believed in. He had a faith…a faith in nature.'

It was then that Grace noticed Gaudi's words carved into the stone wall…

"Those who look for the laws of Nature as a support for their new works collaborate with the creator."

Grace smiled. She felt a warm glow inside.

The sunlight seemed to get more intense. The air was hot and humid, causing beads of sweat to condense on her brow. Then, in an instant, both the church and the old lady vanished. She was alone.

Although by herself, Grace didn't feel afraid. Intuitively she knew something remarkable was about to be revealed to her. She paused for breath and tried to recall the events so far. What message was she supposed to be taking from what she had seen?

She thought about the people the old lady had shown her. C.S. Lewis, Einstein, Gaudi – all people who had achieved great things.

She thought about all of them. And then it came to her. In that moment she knew what connected them. They were all Creators. They all had the capacity to envision what was not yet conceivable to others. They also had the courage to proclaim their vision to the world and so create it. They believed it and then they saw it. This was exactly what the old lady had taught her on the beach.

Grace looked down at her feet despondently. 'But what has this got to do with me? I am not like any of them.' She still didn't believe that any of this had anything to do with her.

'And where are you?' she shouted upwards directing the question to the absent old lady who seemed to have abandoned her.

As she looked up, she noticed the clouds were changing shape. How odd she thought, as an unusual cloud formation appeared. Grace stared. It looked like an arm with a delicately shaped hand and two forefingers intertwined and pointing upwards. I have seen this before, I am sure of it.

She was held captivated by what was unfolding before her eyes. She knew it was a sign and sensed it had some significance but she didn't know what it was telling her.

A thick mist drew in from nowhere and gathered around her, winding upwards from the tip of her toes to the top of her head until she could see nothing. As it began to clear, she found herself standing in front of a large wooden door.

Grace cautiously turned the rusty iron knob and the door creaked open. She blinked a few times trying to focus her eyes in the darkness. She found herself in a large room.

She looked around, feeling like a detective trying to piece a story together. There was no one there but her.

Grace noticed bits and pieces of machinery, tools belonging to an engineer, and lots of architectural drafts close by. She could also see an easel, paint brushes and paints. But her eyes were magnetically drawn to an anatomical sketch of a baby curled in foetal position in a womb. It was an oddly beautiful creation.

Looking around for more clues she noticed a piece of thick parchment paper lying on top of an ornate Italian dresser. It was folded over into a letter or envelope and written across the front in black ink was her name – Grace. A white feather quill lay beside it. This can't be she thought, turning quickly to see who had left it for her. But there was no one there.

Grace picked it up and turned it over. It was embossed with an old fashioned red wax seal in the shape of a keyhole. Grace looked at it for a few minutes, studying it from every angle. Nervously she began to peel back the seal and open it, careful to retain the wax keyhole shape.

Inside was a postcard. It was the *Salvator Mundi*, the exact same card and painting that she had given to the old lady earlier that day.

Grace was shocked. Letting out a gasp, she dropped the card from her hand and it fell onto the wooden floor with a loud clunk.

She picked it up and traced her finger slowly and deliberately around the delicate fingers of the Saviour's hand. It was the cloud formation she had seen earlier in the sky. Grace turned the postcard over and for the second time that day read the quote:

"There are three classes of people: those who see, those who see when they are shown, those who do not see."

Grace somehow knew that all of this; the room, the work, the creative energy that she felt present, was that of one of the greatest Creators ever known… Leonardo da Vinci.

She felt a stillness come over her and a silence so complete she merged with it. Then she remembered there was something else in the letter; she had heard it drop with the card. Looking down, Grace spotted a key lying on the floor. She picked it up and examined it closely. It was very old and surprisingly heavy with intricate baroque swirls at the top. It was mesmerising.

'What is this for?' she asked aloud. No response.

Closing her eyes, Grace asked anxiously. 'What is this key for? Please tell me.'

When she opened her eyes, only a few seconds later, she was astonished to find herself in near darkness. A fragile light seeped eerily from beneath a circular series of twelve doors which surrounded her.

She moved slowly and hesitantly towards the first door. She inserted the key into the lock and turned it. Although she heard a click, the door remained locked.

Moving around the room in a clockwise direction, Grace attempted to unlock each door in sequence but with no success. As she reached the final door, she thought to herself, this must be it for sure, but again the door remained locked.

Losing her patience, Grace banged on the wooden door in frustration. Giving the door one final, angry strike, she shouted, 'What is this key for?' and punched the air with her fist. She gripped the key so tightly that it hurt, and as she unfurled her clenched fist she saw a perfect imprint of the key on the palm of her hand.

She began to scream almost hysterically and repeated the question over and over. Finally, throwing herself onto the ground she began to cry a stream of tears that wouldn't stop flowing. Huge wracking sobs tore through her whole body.

'Please tell me what to do. Help me. I just want to go home. Please, please get me out of this dream.'

Then from nowhere, a voice whispered in her ear, 'Grace, *believe* and you will see.'

She stopped suddenly and looked up. There was no-one there. Had she heard a voice? Grace was afraid. 'Who is this?'

The voice spoke again. 'Life will always present locked doors, Grace, but when you **Ask**, you will receive the answer. And when you **Believe**, you will see.'

'What are you talking about?' she stammered faintly.

The voice continued. 'Do you still believe you have nothing to do with Creation, Grace?'

'I don't know. I am not sure. I am not like any of them.' Grace sobbed. 'I think I am going crazy. I want to know what all of this means. I want to know why I am here.' She gulped back her tears.

'Quiet, little one' the voice responded firmly but with compassion. 'You have to believe and then you will see.' The voice disappeared and she was alone again.

Grace eventually stood up, composed herself and walked forward to try the locks again. For some strange reason, she believed that something would be different this time. She had no idea why. It was then she noticed a box sitting at the foot of one of the doors.

'How could I have missed this?' The box was really quite large.

She thought again about the voice and Leonardo's quote. Even when she was shown something, she still didn't see; she missed it, totally. She suddenly became aware that she had been doing that all of her life.

Grace picked the box up and ran her fingers over the top. It was beautiful. It had a strange texture to it, a mixture of wood and thick canvas. There was a picture of an old man on the box dressed in long flowing robes and carrying scrolls of paper. He looked like a messenger.

Grace saw a keyhole at the side of the box. She took a deep breath in through her nose and then slowly exhaled, feeling her breath move up from her stomach and out through her mouth. She believed that her key would open the box.

As she turned the key, a feeling which could only be described as pure love flooded her body. She felt it deep within her heart. She felt safe. The box opened effortlessly as she believed it would. Inside she found a scroll of thick paper tied with a red ribbon. Grace untied the ribbon and uncurled the paper. Written in the same beautiful hand writing as her letter, were the words:

I Am a Creator.

Closing her eyes, she hugged the scroll tightly to her chest and said 'I am a creator.' Grace was unsure of the significance of the words. But as she spoke them out loud, a curious power surged through her.

CHAPTER 8

JUST ASK

Grace woke up from her dream with a start. She quickly looked around to see where she was.

The old lady was sitting calmly drinking tea. 'Great, you're back. Meet anyone interesting?' she asked mischievously, laughing loudly.

'Did that really happen to me?' Grace wasn't sure if it was a dream or if it was real.

She then began to give the old lady a brief synopsis of her encounters and described the scroll with the words "I Am a Creator" inscribed on it.

'Is it true? Creation? That I am a Creator?'

'Yes it is, Grace. When you believe it is' the old lady said.

Grace thought about the four famous Creators. Up until now she had believed that these people were very special and very different from her. They were people she admired, great people who had created extraordinary things that had changed the world. She had been in awe of their ability.

But now she was beginning to believe that all of this potential was available to her too.

Grace noticed that although what each of them had created was very different; they all had incredible vision, imagination and a powerful belief in what they were doing. But she had also noticed something else; there was a common thread that weaved its way through their creativity. Grace recognised that what they were doing, whether it was writing, creating, painting, inventing or designing, it had meaning. It was important to them.

'Well done, Grace, what a great observation you have made. Yes, it is true. The Creators found their purpose. Creation is easier when you find something fulfilling to do or to be; when you tap into your life purpose.'

Grace thought deeply for a moment and her eyes began to fill with tears. 'But how do you find purpose? What if you don't know what you are supposed to be doing with your life?' Grace asked with genuine concern in her voice. 'I have no idea what my purpose is?'

The old lady nodded. 'Yes, not knowing what your purpose is can be a challenge.'

She took Grace's hands and cradled them in hers. Looking deep into her eyes she said 'So what you need to do is "Ask". If there's anything you want to know, just "Ask". It's simple Grace.'

Grace was confused. 'Ask? Ask who?'

The old lady got up from her chair and moved across the room to a bookcase and lifted a large, heavy book from the shelf. She flicked through pages which had been carefully bent back with clear markings against things of significance. She pointed out a passage to Grace.

"For everyone who asks, receives. Those who seek, find, and to those who knock, the door will be opened."

The old lady put the book down on the table in front of her and said, 'Grace, if you wanted to understand how an invention worked, who would you ask?'

Grace hesitated, 'The inventor?'

'Yes, of course. It's obvious isn't it? The one who created the invention.' The old lady was smiling. 'Grace, we are connected to an infinite creative intelligence which knows all of the answers. We need only Ask.'

'Really?' Grace raised her eyebrows at this notion.

'Do you have a computer, Grace?'

'Are you kidding? My laptop is practically part of me!' Grace said, remembering just how much time she spent on her notebook.

'Okay. Your computer runs on a programme, which is written in a complex code. Agreed?' the old lady asked.

'Do you ever doubt that there is a programmer behind the intelligence of your computer? Someone who created the code and understands everything about it?'

Grace listened intently still unsure of where all of this was going.

'So why then would we not believe that there is also an intelligent mind behind everything created in our world?'

'Grace, the universal programmer is conscious, it knows everything. It created everything, including you! It knows all the answers to every question. You need only *Ask*.'

'Yes, I see. That makes sense' Grace was starting to understand.

To emphasise the point, the old lady finished by saying, 'The key is to be open to this possibility and not to be defensive.'

'Grace, your heart and soul are connected to this intelligence; and so they know what's right for you. Seek this connection within. The answers are within you. Be mindful of your question but never dwell on it too much or stress yourself about getting an immediate response. Be patient with yourself and trust. The answers will come. Answers come from everywhere, inside and out.'

The old lady smiled and it warmed Grace's heart.

Grace recalled how she had asked about the purpose of the key when she was in Leonardo's workshop. She realised that it was then that she had heard the voice and was guided to the answer.

The old lady stood up and Grace followed, taking it to mean that it was time to leave. She suddenly noticed something glistening on the carpet. She picked it up. It was a smooth, shiny translucent pebble. Inside it held a tiny rainbow, its beautiful colours emanating through the hardness of the stone.

'Take it with you to remind you to always Ask' the old lady said. Grace turned the small stone over in her hand several times, closed her eyes and squeezed it tightly. She then slipped it inside her pocket.

The old lady added, 'Grace, you need to understand what makes your heart sing. This is different for everyone. You have to find out what is right for you. The key is to discover what is written in your heart. We can chat more about this next Saturday.'

With that, the old lady embraced her and kissed her goodbye.

Grace felt happy. She skipped through the garden under the watchful eye of the chunky robin, pulled open the heavy wooden door and closed it carefully behind her.

The bus arrived just as Grace reached the bus stop. It was the same driver.

'Excellent timing!' Grace said.

'Yes, it always is. You just need to Ask!' said the bus driver with a knowing smile.

CHAPTER 9

HEART'S DESIRE

The flat was quiet apart from the steady tick-tock of the grand-daughter clock in the hall and the whirling wind outside.

Giant raindrops flowed down the windows in rivulets, racing each other down the bevelled panes before merging into one at the end of their journey on the windowsill. Grace was fascinated; she loved the rain and had done so ever since she was a little girl.

Her attention moved on to the one question that had continued to niggle at her. She could not shift it from her thoughts. 'What is it that I am here to create?' Grace had been asking all that week but had received no answers. She decided that she would ask the old lady why this was when she saw her later that day.

The bus journey was like a Star Trek teleporter. Grace appeared to have arrived at her destination almost instantaneously.

She entered the cobbled lane and headed for the old lady's house, but before she reached the big wooden doors, she noticed a skinny man with unusually long legs striding towards her wearing a pinstriped suit. He was carrying a tower-high pile of books and papers and seemed to be in a dreadful hurry. As he passed, Grace accidently clipped him with her bag causing his mini library to fly up into the air and scatter from one end of the lane to the other. 'Oh, I'm so sorry' Grace apologised, 'I don't know how that happened' and she quickly began to pick the books and papers up from the ground.

As she lifted up the last book, she stared in wonder at the word on its cover. It read "Grace" designed beautifully with delicate gold leaf calligraphy. The tall man peered down at her through small-rimmed bi-focal glasses. He looked a bit out of place, as if he had come from another era.

'I believe that book is meant for you, Grace.'

He knows my name too?

Still awestruck from what had just happened Grace stuttered 'Thank you. Do I know you?' but as she looked up he was gone.

Grace opened "The Book" to find it completely empty apart from one sentence. *It all starts with a blank page…a space to create.*

Unnerved and more than a little confused, Grace glanced at her watch, realising that she was now late. She slipped "The Book" into her bag.

The heavy wooden door to the garden was ajar. Grace entered and walked directly to the gate. She was flabbergasted to see the old lady completing a series of somersaults on the lawn.

What on earth is going on? Grace said to herself as the old lady continued her display, seemingly oblivious to Grace's presence. She was wearing a multi-coloured leotard with diamanté encrusted shoulders and small white pumps with elastic criss-crossing around her tiny feet. Performing somersaults, backflips, mid-air twists and all sorts of gymnastic movements, she finished victoriously throwing both her arms into the air as if she had just won an Olympic medal.

Grace was astonished. But the old lady just smoothed down her hair and walked casually over to where Grace was standing.

'Ah, there you are. I was just doing my morning routine. Come in, the kettle's on' she said.

Yeah! Like it's perfectly normal for an old woman to be doing gymnastics on the lawn in the morning! I mean, what age is she anyway? Grace thought to herself smiling. She loved this old lady and her quirkiness.

They sat down for tea and the old lady brought out a cake stand bearing a pyramid of Tunnock's Teacakes. Grace picked one off the top spot and carefully opened the shiny red and silver foil wrapper. She held the little dome biscuit in her hand and began to peel away the chocolate with her teeth, revealing the white, sticky mallow underneath which she scooped up with her tongue before finally finishing off the soft crumbly biscuit bottom. She couldn't make up her mind what part of the biscuit she liked the best.

Grace realised the old lady was staring at her with raised eyebrows. 'Goodness, what an odd way to eat a Tunnock's Teacake!'

Grace giggled loudly before replying 'That's rich coming from someone who does somersaults in her garden wearing a sparkly leotard!'

The old lady did not respond. Instead she picked up the biscuit's foil wrapper, placed it down on the table and carefully spread it out. She began to rub the wrinkled surface with the side of her delicate thumb until the shiny silver foil was as smooth as glass. The old lady then turned to Grace and let out a huge satisfied sigh and said 'I believe this is the best part of a Tunnock's Teacake, Grace!' and began to laugh.

Grace admired how the old lady was able to laugh at herself freely. It occurred to Grace that this was something that she was never really able to do, she was too self-conscious.

As they began to talk more seriously Grace asked the question which had been causing her angst all week. 'What am I supposed to be creating?'

The old lady seemed to ignore the question and instead said 'Tell me Grace, does your head ever get full of chatter?'

Grace nodded. 'Yes, I wake up every morning and go to bed every night with a head full of chatter; things to do, things not done, and things I shouldn't have done!' She felt anxious and exhausted just talking about it. 'It's painful, but I don't know how to stop it happening.'

'Here, sit on this' and the old lady threw a round purple and gold silk cushion onto the floor. It looked Indian, embroidered with gold threads and dazzling with rainbow mirrored sequins.

The old lady then walked over to an antique record player and pulled a shiny black vinyl record from a faded cardboard sleeve. She carefully placed it on the turntable and Grace could hear the sound of the needle as it traced the grooves. The record crackled in a comforting, nostalgic way.

The old lady threw another cushion on the floor and sat down cross-legged.

'We're going to meditate' she said.

Okay, thought Grace, bemused, I'll just go with this, and following the old lady's lead, sat on her cushion and crossed her legs too.

She closed her eyes and attempted to empty the rubbish from her head. Grace struggled at first as silly, random and totally mundane thoughts drifted in and out. She noticed how repetitive they were.

Grace listened to the rhythmic, pulsing music. The music touched her. Although her eyes were closed, she imagined that she could see and feel the individual notes dancing around the room in a carefully co-ordinated sequence. She seemed to be absorbing their vibration as they moved through her. She was relaxed and at peace; she felt free.

Grace found herself rising. Up and up she went, floating higher and higher towards outer space. She circled around the planets, close enough to touch the stars. It was so peaceful and such an incredibly beautiful feeling. She wanted to stay there forever.

As the music stopped, Grace knew that she must return, and did so reluctantly. Slowly she opened her eyes.

The old lady was holding a small Tibetan singing bowl made from what looked like a copper or nickel alloy. It had symbols embossed lightly on the inside. She began to run a wooden stick around the rim and as she did so, the bowl came to life. The tiny high pitched vibration grew and grew until it sounded like a choir of angels that had been summoned to sing from inside the bowl.

Allowing the sound to fade to a natural end, the old lady placed the bowl down on a little green cushion with golden tassles and coloured beads at each corner. She looked at Grace and said 'If you really want to find out what you are here to create, you have to let everything go. Empty your mind. Be still and ask, and then you will know.'

'Listen to your heart, Grace. This is where you will find your treasure and the answers to your heart's desire.'
Breaking a rather pleasant silence Grace asked 'Isn't desire a bad thing to have? We are not supposed to have desires, or so I was told.'

The old lady smiled. 'Firstly, desire is not a bad thing at all. We are brought up to believe that it is wrong and that it should be suppressed. This is a distortion of the truth and confuses the thing desired with desire itself. Desire is as natural as breathing. It is the inner longing of the soul. Nothing can be created without the energy of desire. It lies behind every thought, action and word we say.'

The old lady took a sip of fragrant tea and continued, 'When you find your heart's desire, you are on the path to your purpose.'

Grace felt the truth of what she was being told.

The old lady continued 'Secondly, people speak about burning desire, having a *burning desire* for something. These are true words because desire is the fuel that lights the fire. Desire is the fire, the inspiration from within that propels you forward. It is the energy that makes you grow and flourish.'

Grace instantly had a vision of a single rosebud bathed in sunshine. It stood proud and was slowly beginning to open, its petals gently spreading into an inspired bloom of colour. It was yellow; she adored yellow roses.

'I am telling you, Grace, desire is an extremely potent force of nature. It is the very source of nature itself. Desire releases the human spirit and it draws to you the thing desired or the elements that comprise the thing desired. In Aramaic, desire is translated as, "of the father", it is a God given longing. So you see desire works within the laws of Creation itself.'

Grace felt herself being inexplicably drawn towards the old lady. She actually felt as if her whole body was moving closer with every word.

'But we often allow other people's judgments or beliefs to douse the fire; we allow them to pour water on our dreams. We listen and believe when they say, "Who said you could do that?" or "You can't do this" or "You'll never be able to do that." We compromise our desires to keep people happy or in response to their limiting beliefs.'

Grace's heart sank.

She spent a lot of her time and energy trying to please people, trying to justify herself or overcoming their doubts and fears. It was exhausting and more often than not left her feeling resentful. It never ended in happiness. How often had she heard negative words from people, listened to them, and believed them to be true? It went right back to her childhood and had continued into her adult life.

Grace remembered every negative word. She could feel them. Each one adding another little layer of armour to keep her away from her dreams and her true self.

'I understand' said Grace. 'I understand all of this. It happened to me and it's still happening.'

The old lady looked at Grace and understood too.

'What happens if you're feeling dead inside and there is no fire? How do you re-light it? How do you get it back?' Grace almost pleaded for an answer.

'There is no getting it back Grace. It is always there, deep in the very heart of you, patiently waiting. You just have to find a way to remove the blocks that have extinguished it.'

'But how? How do I do that?' Grace sounded frantic.

The old lady gently took Grace's face in her hands and said 'By accepting and letting go, Grace.'

'By accepting where you are right now, by letting go of any fear, anger, bitterness or disappointment. By letting go of all unhelpful and negative emotions, you create a space and allow new feelings and experiences to come in. Desire, true desire, comes from a divine place of inspiration, hope and happiness. So it is important to create that environment to allow your desires to develop, then your heart will be unlocked and you will be free to create and live your purpose.'

The old lady smiled. 'And you will know when you have found it. Your heart knows its true desire. It desires you too. It longs to know you again. And when you find each other, your heart will sing a song of love and joy.'

They both sat in silence for a while. 'Trust your instincts, Grace. Pay attention to what you feel in every situation and you will instinctively know which path to choose. Trust.'

Grace understood. A deep inner knowing caused the hairs on the back of her neck to stand on end.

'Tell me more, please' Grace asked, like a child wanting another bedtime story.

The old lady gave her a loving smile. 'Have you ever been so engaged in something that you have lost all sense of time? Or you were so connected with what you were doing that you forgot everything else around you?'

Grace thought long and hard 'Yes, as a child, watching raindrops race down my window.'

'What a perfect answer, Grace. Our purpose is simply to do whatever makes us most happy. Something that we love. This isn't complicated stuff you know!'

Grace sat still in quiet reflection. There was a comfortable silence between them.

'Remember, Grace. Love is the true source of your desire.'

'But there is a challenge with this. It comes from fear. Fear blocks our desires. Fear destroys love. When the flow of desire is blocked we start to wither and wilt and our dreams shrivel up and die. And with this, we lose the most important part of ourselves...our purpose.'

The old lady saw Grace's reaction to this and said 'Oh don't worry, Grace. Next week I will teach you something really powerful that will help you remove any doubts and fears and allow all of your desires to flow to you.' Grace felt relieved.

As she sat on the bus on her way home, she took out "The Book" that she had picked up when she bumped into the tall man earlier that day. She looked at the cover and then gently traced her finger around her name. Grace somehow knew that she would soon understand what she had been longing for all of these years, and learn what she was supposed to be creating. She felt a peculiar tingle in her heart.

CHAPTER 10

MAGIC BUTTONS

Unlocking your heart's desire and discovering your purpose. This was a new and exciting possibility for Grace. But just as quickly as the excitement arrived, her mind reverted back to its more familiar groove riddled with worry, doubt and fear.

She had some pressing questions that she wanted to ask the old lady, and upon arrival, began interrogating her almost immediately.

'I know I said that I believed that I am a Creator but one thing really bothers me. Do I create the things that I don't want in my life?'

'What a great question' said the old lady, completely unperturbed. 'Let me explain exactly how this works. You see Grace, everything begins with a thought. If we keep focusing on those thoughts, we attach feelings and emotions to them. As thoughts and emotions are creative, the subject of those thoughts will "show up" through time. That's what happened with my deckchair. Remember?'

'Yes. I understand that' replied Grace. 'But say, for example, I believe that I'm not good enough and I put myself down? Or if I think that I will fail at something or that someone else would be much better at doing something than me? Or what if I'm not feeling great about myself or I am blaming myself or feeling shame for things that have happened in my past?' Grace was feeling concerned about the possibility that every negative thought she had would become real. 'You know... those kinds of things? Am I creating those things too?'

The old lady responded bluntly 'Yes, you are', and continued, 'Every thought is the cause and every condition the effect; now can you see how important it is to be aware of your thoughts, Grace?'

Grace felt very anxious.

The old lady stood up and walked over to a cupboard in the corner of the room. Lifting out a huge tartan shawl she draped it around her tiny frame.

The tartan was unusually vibrant. It lifted the mood in the room instantly. Grace had never seen a tartan like it before. It was like a huge mass of purple heather, thistles and bluebells shot through with lime greens and a touch of shocking pink. The effect against the old lady's grey hair was stunning.

Distracted, Grace forgot about her negative thoughts as she focused her attention on the beauty of the shawl.

'Enjoy the present moment, Grace.'

'Too often we spend our time worrying about the past and then worrying about the future. We miss the colourful and precious moments in our life right now. It is so important to be present.'

Grace nodded. She knew how much she worried, all the time. Anything and everything. She took a deep breath and relaxed, finding her calm again.

The old lady continued. 'Everything that is in your world, you have created on some level. Do you see how powerful we are?'

'Now, back to your question about why anyone would want to create negative things in their life.' The old lady threw part of her shawl over her right shoulder and said matter-of-factly, 'They don't.'

Grace was puzzled.

'We are creating all of the time, Grace. But bizarrely, we also bring those things we don't want into our lives. This is because we create non-deliberately. We create without being consciously aware of it.'

'You see, everything starts as a thought .... including worries, which are simply thoughts about things we don't want, and here is what people do. They think about these worries and play them over and over in their minds. Often they share their worries with other people. Great idea, isn't it...share the worry!' The old lady laughed.

Grace agreed. 'Yes, it is ridiculous when you think about it that way' and she laughed too.

'Then they start to imagine it, creating a picture of "the alleged catastrophe" in their mind's eye. Some people are great at this part; they even visualise the event as if it were actually happening!'

The old lady was on a roll. 'And if they do that for long enough, they begin to feel it. And guess what happens next? When they feel it, they believe it and as you now know Grace, believing is seeing. And so, it becomes their reality. It's The Creation Process. Can you see how powerful this is?'

The old lady continued.

'But it's the feelings behind these thoughts, where the real creative power lies. To help you understand this idea, let me share some science with you. Did you know that I'm a scientist, Grace?'

'Yes, you mentioned that.' Grace chuckled, remembering the old lady had told her this on the beach.

'There's lots of science within The Creation Process.'

'Think of our emotions, our feelings as energy waves' the old lady looked up, trying to find a good analogy. 'Exactly!' she said to herself out loud, as if someone had just spoken to her and given her the answer. 'Like radio frequencies.'

'You transmit them and you receive them. Your emotions are energy waves with a vibration and a frequency.' The old lady continued. 'There are only two types of vibration, positive and negative. If you're experiencing positive emotions, you will send out positive vibrations and create positive things around you. If you're experiencing negative feelings, you will be sending out negative energy waves and will create negative things around you. Your emotions are magnetic. It's a universal law. It really is that simple.'

'Did you know there are over three thousand five hundred emotions in the dictionary? I should know. I have counted them!

Grace just nodded in agreement, thinking about the time it would take to verify the old lady's claim.

'But when it comes right down to it, there are only two that really matter. **"Love"** and **"Fear"**. Think of it as one long emotional continuum, Grace. At one end is love and at the other end fear. These two are the most powerful emotions we can have. All the rest are in between. When we create out of love, only good can come of it. But sadly most people create from fear.' The old lady paused for a moment. 'Most people spend the majority of their time focusing on fearful and destructive emotions. And that, my dear, is why most people are creating what they don't want. Destroying all of the magnificent possibilities of life and completely unaware that they have anything to do with it.'

Grace's eyes widened. She was becoming aware of the implications of all of this, remembering her own self-imposed emotional roller coaster life.

The old lady jumped up suddenly full of excitement, and throwing her hands into the air exclaimed 'Grace, the great news is, that it works just as easily the other way around too!'

'We can use this exact same creative process, only this time positively. By thinking positive thoughts and choosing positive emotions instead, we can create deliberately and positively.' The old lady continued. 'The other great news is that Creation doesn't happen instantly. It can take time. Thankfully, we have time to work on our negative thoughts and reset them to something much more positive, which can stop the negative things from being created.'

Grace felt a massive sense of relief.

The old lady turned and looked directly at her. 'Do you know anyone in life who says things like, *This always happens to me, that would never happen to me…why me*?'

Grace did. In fact she didn't have to think too long. Her cheeks flushed pink knowing that she said those very same things to herself almost all of the time. She looked down and shuffled her feet uncomfortably.

'Grace, instead of things happening **to you**, things can happen **by you**. It's all about awareness. It's about becoming aware of what you are thinking and feeling and then doing something deliberate to change it. Begin to notice what you are thinking and how you are feeling and if it doesn't feel good, choose again.'

There was so much for Grace to think about. Her head was reeling.

'Think about awareness. It simply means being conscious of what is going on, in and around you. It's about becoming acutely aware of your thoughts and your feelings and what frequency you are on. It is so important.

'If you are stuck on a negative frequency, you can change it. We are just energy. And our energy can change easily. Once you realise this you don't have to be stuck in negative energy anymore.'

'Wait here. I have something to show you' said the old lady. She went back over to the cabinet which had housed her shawl and this time brought out a multi-coloured, cube shaped box. She put it down right in front of Grace on a small table.

'Open it', the old lady said.

Grace looked at it for a moment in puzzlement. She wondered what it was. Mystified, she started to giggle like a little girl.

'Is this a trick?' Grace leaned over cautiously, picked it up and released the clasp. The lid of the box sprang open like a jack-in-the-box. But what popped out wasn't a scary clown, it was an enormous rainbow button on a gold spring.

The button had one word written across it in big, bold capital letters. 'RESET.'

The old lady laughed, leaned over and pushed the button back into the box.

'Here, open it again' she said, clearly enjoying every moment of this.

Grace opened the lid again but this time, to her surprise, instead of a rainbow button, a huge–tartan button popped up and the drone of Scottish bagpipes immediately filled the air.

The two women laughed hysterically.

'This is what I do whenever I have a negative thought or feeling. I recognise it for what it is. It is just a thought, that has created a feeling, which is just energy. Then I press my magic button and "RESET". When I reset or change my thought from a negative thought to a positive one, I change my feelings and my frequency. And as a result, I change my "Creation Set Point." This resets my possibilities and my future, but this time, I create positively.'

The old lady paused and stared directly into Grace's hazel eyes. There was complete silence.

'But here is the key, Grace. The moment I choose to "RESET" I am making that choice in the **present** moment. It is always in the **present** moment that I create from.'

The old lady relaxed back into her seat with a huge satisfied smile. She was especially happy that she had been able to take such a complex subject and make it easy for Grace to understand.

Grace looked at the big RESET button and smiled. She was also pleased that the old lady's explanation had a happy ending.

The old lady patted Grace's hand, 'Remember, you always have your magic RESET button.'

Grace loved this present.

She started to think about where and when she would use it. She could use it whenever there was doubt or fear, tiredness or anger, anxiety or hurt. Whenever she didn't feel good enough, she could now just press her magic jack-in-the-box RESET button and shift her state of being instantly. Moment by moment.

The old lady looked at Grace. 'Well, what do you think? Does it all make sense to you?'

'Yes, it does. It's genius.' Grace was genuinely excited by its endless possibilities.

'That's good. I am happy for you, Grace.'

'Remember,' the old lady said 'You are always creating. If you don't like what you have created, RESET and choose again.'

CHAPTER 11

THE LIBRARY

It had been a few weeks since she had seen the old lady and she had butterflies in her stomach as she dressed for her visit.

She picked up "The Book" which was sitting on her dressing table and whispered its title, 'Grace.' Images suddenly flashed through her mind of the strange man in the lane, with the pinstripe suit, who appeared and then disappeared. "The Book" with no content, and the conversations with the old lady about desire, purpose and Creation, all danced together in her imagination. They instantly created a perfect symphony, full of the magic of her unwritten future.

'Creation. What is it I am here to create?' She spoke the words out loud and then wrote them on the first page of her book. 'There you go, that's my Ask' she said, a little embarrassed that she was talking to empty space. But she also recognised that this process of asking was becoming easier every time she did it. She decided to be open and optimistic about receiving an answer.

Grace felt energised and supported by her new thoughts and beliefs, especially now that she had her magical jack–in–the-box, RESET button to assist.

As she waited for the bus, she became aware that she was looking forward to seeing the driver again. When the bus arrived she stepped inside and was immediately greeted with a huge smile. She liked her new friend.

Arriving in the beautiful Victorian walled garden, everything looked even more alive than usual. Plants and flowers were springing to life and a fusion of purple greeted her eyes and the smell of lavender filled her nostrils. A beautiful blue and black butterfly fluttered past her nose and landed on a pink Echinacea flower. Small brightly coloured birds were playing and splashing on an ornate stone bird bath. Grace was acutely aware that all of this was completely out of season. It was as if the garden had its own micro climate.

The old lady appeared on the patio. She looked particularly beautiful today, exhibiting a radiant glow. Grace wondered whether this glow had always been there, or whether she was only now seeing it because of her new sensitivity to energy.

'Come in, come in, how are you?' she smiled.

'I'm good, I am really good.'

Settling down, Grace immediately began to tell the old lady about her heightened senses. 'It's as if I am able to see colour and light and appreciate even the smallest detail.'

The old lady laughed 'That's wonderful, Grace. It means that you are reaching a new level of awareness. Good for you.'

The old lady then stood up and said 'I have a surprise for you, something you are going to love. We have a lot to experience today, so let's get started.'

Grace loved surprises.

The old lady took Grace's hand and held it tightly. The room started to spin, very slowly at first. Grace began to feel light and dizzy. She heard the old lady's voice whispering in her ear 'Love is the supreme Creator.' Grace intuitively let go, the light vanished and everything became dark.

Opening her eyes she found herself in an extraordinary room dominated by huge bookcases with glass doors. Intricately carved wooden pillars and walls supported an antique ceiling decorated with wood paneling and cornicing framed with coats of arms. The ceiling stood thirty majestic feet above her. She was in an old library and it was astonishingly beautiful.

As the sun beamed through the enormous windows, the stained glass projected a rainbow image of the Greek philosophers Virgil and Homer onto the antique floor. Grace sensed that she was in a monastery or convent, or somewhere equally spiritual. She could hear the faint echo of voices in quiet prayer and feel love and faith in the very fabric of the walls.

As she ran her hand over one of the bookcases, her eyes exploring the wonder before her, she whispered 'So much knowledge and wisdom.'

The books looked ancient, written in secret places and passed down through time. Grace tried to open some of the bookcases but they were all securely locked. Glancing around she noticed a tiny heart shaped silver casket which, when opened, revealed a minute key sitting on a small burgundy velvet cushion.

She picked it up with her forefinger and thumb and looked about her. Remembering to Ask, she closed her eyes, cleared her mind and imagined opening the bookcase with the key.

With her eyes shut lightly she began to run her hand over the bookcases until she found one which seemed to be vibrating ever so slightly. Her middle finger caught on something rough and uneven; opening her eyes she peered down into a tiny void.

Grace knew instinctively that she had found the one. She held the key up to her lips, kissed it and felt its warmth. She placed it inside the lock; it fitted perfectly. Turning it carefully she heard a tiny click and the lock released, opening the door.

Grace could never have anticipated what happened next.

The books inside began to jump from the shelves. One by one they leapt out, whizzed past her head and formed an untidy collection as they fell to the floor. 'What on earth? How did that happen?' she gasped as she stood in disbelief staring down at the pile of books near her feet.

Her thoughts were quickly interrupted as she heard the old lady laugh behind her as she said 'Ah, that's excellent. They found you, Grace.'

'They found me? You knew all about this? You were here all along?'

'Just because you can't see me doesn't mean I am not there' the old lady said. 'I am always around, I will always be here. Trust that I will be nearby whenever you need me. I love watching you learn, Grace.'

'Thank you' mumbled Grace. She felt slightly embarrassed but she also liked the idea of having someone around to teach her and to look out for her. She couldn't remember that ever happening before. In that moment Grace had a feeling that the old lady was her teacher but what was she being taught?

The old lady bent down, 'Right, let's clear this up. These books have waited a long time to be read.'

They worked together, picking up the books and arranged them neatly on the floor. The old lady then scattered some cushions down and threw a furry faux leopard-skin blanket over the top. 'Let's sit here for a while' she said.

Grace looked around her and said 'I love it here.'

'There is much to love. This is my library, Grace. I am the steward of these books and a teacher of the ancient knowledge that they hold.'

Grace was shocked. Only seconds ago she had that very thought, and asked the question. Had the old lady read her mind?

The old lady picked up the first book. 'These are very precious, Grace. Let's explore them together, one by one. Each one holds a message for you, each a different chapter from the same story.'

Grace felt her heart begin to beat faster and she moved closer. The student was ready to learn.

CHAPTER 12

THE SPIRIT OF ADVENTURE

Grace picked up the first book and opened it; an intense ray of light burst outward and filled the room. The entire Universe was being released from within the book's pages. Planets spun into the air, stars shot across the room and the moon orbited a sun that exploded into the space between Grace and the old lady. Planet Earth landed on her lap. She picked it up and leaned forward to examine it. Grace saw tiny boats sail across the world's seas and trains steam across the vast continents. She felt herself being drawn at great speed from outer space into the little Earth which was now nestled in the palm of her hand.

Grace found herself standing in a desert. She scanned full circle but could see nothing but sand. Dunes the size of small mountains rolled like golden waves before her.

She became aware of a faint vibration beneath her feet which then intensified to a regular heavy pulsating rhythm. Grace looked to the horizon and saw a piebald horse and rider galloping toward her. Within moments the rider, a tall slim black woman, deftly pulled her mount alongside Grace. Her hair, sectioned into numerous braids was intertwined with an assortment of beads. Necklaces made from colourful shells and feathers hung around her neck in various lengths. Near naked, she was swathed only in a duck egg blue cloth which swirled around her like a giant flag, heralding the importance of her arrival.

Grace could sense something wild and adventurous about her.

The woman jumped agilely from her horse. She untied a leather sack which hung just beside her saddle, pulled out a flask of water and poured it into the ground. Instead of being absorbed into the hot desert sand, the water began to expand and grow, spreading until it formed a large pool from which the horse immediately began to drink.

The woman returned to her saddle bag and pulled out what looked to be a handful of seeds. She tossed these into the air and as they landed she began to spread them out, her dark hands, adorned with silver rings and bracelets, expertly working them into the barren land. Magically, life began to sprout from the sand. A tiny shoot grew into a tall tree which generously spread its leafy branches to make a welcome shade in the heat of the sun.

The woman sat down under nature's canopy, looked up to the sky and gave thanks. She continued to pull objects out from her bag. Wood, a compass, books, journals, maps and finally a globe exactly like the one Grace held in her hand. It started to radiate light and Grace could see right through to its core. She could see continents, countries, cities, buildings and people. She observed explorers and pioneers from every age as they left the known and travelled far and wide in search of new lands and cultures.

Rain began to pour through the clouds trapped inside the transparent orb cleansing and nourishing it. The most wondrous double rainbow was created which arced 360° and orbited the micro Earth.

Leaving the globe to one side, the woman lifted her robe and drew a knife from a leather sheath that was tied around her thigh. She took the piece of wood and started carving. When she had finished she threw the wood high up into the air. Grace looked up; it seemed to hover in space for a moment before suddenly falling back down to earth and landing directly into Grace's outstretched hand. The wood bore the inscription…

"Only when you are prepared to venture into the unknown, will you create a world of magical possibility."

Grace clasped it tightly in her hands and closed her eyes, imagining a world full of possibility. Her skin tingled with excitement.

Suddenly she was back in the library and sitting beside the old lady. The wooden plaque was still in her hands.

'Who was she?' Grace asked the old lady.

'She was The Spirit of Adventure. She was showing you how small our world is in a vast limitless Universe. We are a small grain of sand in an endless desert, a drop of water in the deepest ocean, a little seed with the DNA of limitless potential locked within. We are the tiniest part of an infinite whole, connected to something quite magnificent, just waiting to be explored.'

The old lady then reflected with sadness on how the majority of people on the planet live ordinary and unhappy lives; trudging along, weighed down by the hopeless drudgery of their own sad journey, resisting the possibilities presented by a constantly evolving and potentially extraordinary life.

Grace turned the wood over in her hands and pondered The Universe. She thought about her part in it and what contribution she was meant to make. She held the wood with both hands, closed her eyes and chose a life full of adventure.

CHAPTER 13

THE MAGICIAN

What were you thinking just there, Grace?' the old lady enquired as Grace placed the first book down on the floor.

Grace enthusiastically told the old lady her thoughts about new possibilities, and the choice she had just made after meeting The Spirit of Adventure. The old lady said 'That is truly magical. Inherent in every choice are the mechanics for its fulfilment. I like your thinking. You're going to love who you're about to meet next, Grace!'

Grace opened the second book. Blue skies, happy voices, children's laughter, coloured balloons and a gigantic ferris wheel; all the sights and sounds of a fun fair. A gilded carousel was rotating elegantly; its riders bobbing up and down in harmony with the music. When Grace looked down she realised that her feet were off the ground and she was actually sitting on one of the painted carousel horses.

Her yellow and gold horse slowly ground to a halt and she noticed a small boy sitting nearby. He had a shock of red unruly hair and a face full of freckles. He was playing with a pack of cards.

Grace jumped down and walked over.

As Grace approached inquisitively, the boy got up from his stool and said 'Hello' and then asked her 'Do you want to pick a card?'

Grace wondered who he was. He looked at her with piercing blue eyes and his intense stare made her feel a little uneasy.

'Actually, you've picked one already. It's the Ace of Hearts, it's in your pocket!' the boy said.

'No, I haven't!' said Grace, as she put her hand in her pocket, only to find herself pulling out a crumpled playing card. It was the Ace of Hearts.

'How did you do that?' she asked him, totally mystified. 'There was no way you could have slipped that inside my pocket without me noticing?'

The boy laughed. 'It's magic' he said with the widest grin, revealing shiny metal braces on his teeth.

'And I notice your watch needs fixed too' and with that he pulled Grace's watch out of his own trouser pocket.

'How did that get there? And how did you know it was broken?' It was true, her watch had stopped recently. Grace was amazed and quite puzzled by this strange young boy.

The boy sat back down and removed a small box of tools from inside his jacket pocket and quickly began dismantling her watch. Cogs and springs and tiny coils flew everywhere. He worked intently for a while, and before Grace knew it, snapped it all back together again, tapped the back of the watch three times, saying 'Abracadabra' and gave it back to her.

'There you are … as good as new.'

Grace took the watch and looked at it. As she pressed it to her ear she couldn't hear a thing.

'Oh it won't work here but once you get back home it will, I promise. You see, I fix things that are broken; a broken watch is without a purpose. People without a purpose are broken, they need fixed too.'

The boy had wisdom beyond his years. Grace was unnerved by this curious child and his magical pockets.

As if on cue, he rummaged in his pockets again, this time removing three purple balls. He began to juggle and, as he did so, the balls transformed into large wooden skittles. Grace stood unblinking, hypnotised by the skittles' rhythmic patterns. Within seconds the skittles had changed again, this time into beautiful white turtle doves which flapped around the boy's head before settling in a flurry of feathers at his feet.

Grace stood astonished, her mouth wide open in disbelief.

'Let me show you this' he said holding up a small jar containing a tiny, fragile grey cocoon. As she looked closely, she saw it move and split open right in front of their eyes. Emerging from within was a delicate lace-like butterfly. Its blue and black wings fluttered, opening and closing as it used them for the very first time. The boy carefully unscrewed the lid and the butterfly flew out, landing on Grace's hand. Its fine gossamer wings blinked in the sunlight. Appearing to gain strength and courage, the butterfly took flight into the bright blue sky.

'People need to change, Grace. Like the butterfly, they need to shed their old skins and allow their old self to die before they can truly live again. Embracing change is the key that will open all doors. When change is swift and without resistance, then and only then will the glorious new unfold.'

The boy took Grace's hand and leading her back towards the carousel said finally 'Grace, it is important for you to understand that everything is either an opportunity to grow or an obstacle to diminish you. What will you choose?'

And with these final words, he let her go and the carousel started moving again, rotating gently. Bright colours flashed before her eyes, everything was spinning, and spinning. Before Grace knew it she was back in the library. She felt dizzy and quickly sat down. The old lady was sitting on the rug drinking tea.

'So what did you make of him? You've just met The Magician.'

'He is fascinating' said Grace.

'Yes he is. He is the master of alchemy and can shape-shift into any form. Watch for his signs. They are everywhere. Sometimes he gets annoyed because we don't see them. He leaves little clues for us all over the place. He wants us to be bold and brave, to evolve. He wants us to listen to our intuition. He is leading people towards their purpose, encouraging them to let go of the old, change and grow.'

Shaking her head, the old lady continued. 'He has a hard job you know. People resist change and ignore the signs, even the most painful and obvious ones, where every cell in their body aches and everything in their world is telling them to shift. But sadly they remain afraid. They stay stuck and broken.'

Grace reached inside her pocket and pulled out the crumpled Ace of Hearts playing card, along with her watch. The hands were moving effortlessly around its tiny face. Something or someone was telling her, that it was now time to fix herself and fix her heart.

CHAPTER 14

A MOTHER'S LOVE

The old woman picked up the third book and a silver white mist rose from its pages shrouding them both with long narrow fingers of vapour. When the mist dissipated they found themselves in a village hall. They could see flags, strips of material and elaborate tapestries depicting dancing figures, golden carriages and elephants. Decorated glass lanterns, home to shimmering candles gave off a warm soft glow.

People were arriving carrying trays of food. A heady spicy aroma filled the air. There were bowls of rice in different colours, pots of curries and stews, and sweet treats. The women wore red and gold saris adorned with precious stones in intricate designs that glittered across the delicate silk fabrics. The men, decked in long white coats with gold embroidery around the edges, wore highly decorated jeweled turbans. Cymbals clashed, music and dance filled the hall. Little children laughed, chasing one another around the room, their elders watching on proudly. The hall was overflowing with joy, happiness and celebration.

The old lady guided Grace quickly beyond all of this and out through a dark velvet curtain at the back of the hall.

Despite the daylight hours it was very dark behind the curtain. There was very little natural sunlight and it was incredibly hot and claustrophobic. Grace put her arms out at each side to feel around her new environment as her eyes had not yet adjusted. Touching the damp walls on either side with her hands she realised they were in a narrow lane.

They slowly made their way along a makeshift cardboard boardwalk which protected them from the mud and dirty water underfoot. The awful smell of the debris of inhumane existence assailed their nostrils.

They passed opening after opening, each covered by a single ragged cloth. As Grace looked up she could see these openings reach at least three stories high and accessed only by the rickety ladders that intermittently lined the walls of the lane. Grace could hear sobs and loud crying.

The old lady stopped and drew back one of the curtains. As they entered Grace saw infant babies and young children being nursed in their mothers' arms. Their small cries were hoarse and painful but no tears fell from their large dark eyes.

Grace noticed a woman in a beautiful white sari. A veil with three blue stripes framed her head. Her sallow skin was deeply wrinkled. Despite the misery of the surrounding scene a bright light emanated from her heart. She was comforting the children and their mothers. Grace knew this was love and she began to cry.

The woman looked up at Grace but said nothing. Grace could sense her extraordinary compassion.

As they exited the small room Grace noticed something fixed to the wall in front of her. It was a small painted tile with an image of a beautiful mother holding a child. A halo of stars encircled the woman's head.

The old lady took Grace's hand, gave it a loving squeeze and then they were back in the library.

Grace was deeply disturbed by what she had seen. 'Why did you show me that?'

'I am showing you contrast, Grace.'

'But it's not fair. Why do some people have so much and others so little? It's wrong.' Grace protested.

'We live in a relative world Grace, where one experience allows us to understand another. Neither of these scenes is right or wrong, good or bad, they just are what they are. If we didn't know sadness we would never understand joy. If we didn't experience poverty we would never know abundance. If we didn't feel fear we would never know love. Without the opposite Grace, we would not be able to understand and know the thing desired.

The old lady continued 'It's how we respond to this that has the greatest importance. Some people are immune to humanity and its contrast. They are emotionally and spiritually disconnected and believe it has nothing to do with them. Contrast gives us a filter to sift the creative from the destructive.'

'The real miracle is when ordinary people use these situations as a catalyst to demonstrate the glory of the human spirit and achieve the greatest feats of service and love.'

Grace reflected on all of this and what it might mean to her and her life. But somehow, her thoughts were distracted by an image of her own mother.

Riddled with guilt and regret Grace began to sob uncontrollably. The old lady cradled her in her arms and rocked her like a baby. 'That's good Grace, let it all out. Crying will remove another little layer that has been keeping you from love.' Grace closed her eyes and cried herself to sleep.

CHAPTER 15

SELF LOVE

When Grace eventually awoke from her sleep the old lady asked 'Would you like to read the last book?' Grace nodded drowsily, still feeling the emotional pain of the previous book's revelations.

As the old lady opened it something fell out. It was a small burnished framed mirror. Grace picked it up and looked at her reflection in it. She looked younger, as if she was looking at herself as a child. As she stared into her own eyes she had an overwhelming feeling of being alone and terribly frightened. Sadness swept over her. She felt a huge desire to reach into the frame, put her arms around this tiny child and just love her.

Grace placed the mirror down. She couldn't look at it anymore, it was too painful. Past hurts were resurfacing. Things that she had chosen to forget. Things she never wanted to feel again. Her eyes filled with tears.

Sensing the mood, the old lady took Grace's hand and encouraged her to begin reading. Grace blinked back her tears, and as she turned the first page she felt them fall into the book. Grace closed her eyes and surrendered.

Putting her hand down she felt the softness of the faux leopard fur blanket beneath her but they were no longer in the library.

They were sitting at the edge of a lake, deep within a forest. A mist covered the treetops making them appear to grow right up and into the clouds themselves.

Grace saw a young girl slowly making her way through the trees. She moved with such amazing grace, as if gliding. Her dark hair was tied neatly in a bun at the nape of her neck. She wore a simple white chiffon dress with a cord made from the same fabric tied in a bow around her tiny waist. The girl was stunningly beautiful.

Grace felt a sense of impending doom. She gripped the old lady's forearm and looked at her nervously. The old lady seemed unperturbed.

The young girl kept walking until she reached the water's edge where she loosened her long dark hair, allowing it to cascade down her back. She took off her sandals and arranged them neatly on the ground. Looking ahead she walked straight into the water until her head disappeared beneath the surface.

Grace couldn't help herself. She cried out, 'Stop, Stop!' but the girl could neither see her nor hear her. Grace turned and looked at the old lady, and in a fit of panicked desperation pleaded 'Please do something. Quick! She is going to drown!'

'It's okay, Grace. Everything is exactly as it should be' the old lady said calmingly.

Just then another woman appeared from behind the trees. Grace did a double take. The woman's hair was grey and her skin wrinkled, but it became immediately apparent to Grace that she was looking at an older version of the girl. But how could this be?

Without any hesitation the older woman walked straight into the water. Just as the girl was about to draw her last breath the woman tenderly put her hands behind the girl's neck and legs, lifted her up and carried her ashore.

The woman held the young girl in her arms. She stroked her wet hair and intermittently wiped the tears from the girl's porcelain face. They sat in silence for what seemed like an eternity.

Grace sat quietly as tears ran down her own cheeks as she watched.

The girl and the woman continued to hold each other tightly, breathing in unison until miraculously their bodies merged, two figures had become one.

The older woman stood up and slipped her sandals on. She then took a white lily which had been fastened in her hair and placed it on the water. As she watched it float gently out and away from her, her wrinkled skin appeared to smooth and her eyes softened. She stood quietly for a few minutes staring out across the water, smiled, and then walked slowly back into the forest disappearing from sight.

The old lady took the book from Grace's hands and closed it gently. As she did so they were immediately back in the library.

Grace was still visibly shaken. 'What does it mean?' Her eyes glistened with tears.

The old lady explained. 'The older woman had spent much of her adult life in pain, caused by her thoughts and beliefs about herself that had originated in her teenage years. Although outwardly beautiful, inside the woman felt ugly and unworthy. She couldn't love or respect herself, and carried this hurt with her into her adult years.'

'What you saw today, Grace, was a ceremony. When you saw the two women merge into one, the older woman was embracing the parts of herself that she had never been able to love. When she took the flower from her hair and let it go, symbolically, she was *letting go* of all of the sadness, fear and shame she had been holding onto from a very young age. The woman was then reborn to herself in love.'

'Finding love doesn't always come about in the way most people think. Finding love is about finding the things that stop love expressing itself through you, and then having the courage to examine them and let them go. Those things are not you, Grace. You are love.'

'To create a full and glorious life, you have to return to love. We create out of love. Love is the supreme Creator.'

Grace felt power in what she was being taught by the old lady. She thought about the small girl she had seen in the mirror earlier and wished that she could find a way to let go.

With this thought Grace felt pain surge through her from the very core of her being.

CHAPTER 16

MIRROR MIRROR

Her eyes were red and puffy and she had broken out in a rash, it was as if something was working itself out of her. Grace studied her face in the mirror. She looked tired; in fact she looked completely exhausted. She hadn't made it into work all week.

In some ways her adventures in the library had left her feeling lighter, as if a burden was beginning to lift. But as the week had progressed, and she had time to reflect on the whole experience, she had begun to feel anxious and frightened.

Old thoughts, feelings and issues from her past were bubbling up from deep within her, huge elephants of emotional pain. It was as if the books and their revelations had been a catalyst for a seismic shift in her emotions. Years of unresolved issues, damage and regret left a raw, visceral pain. She felt incredibly exposed and vulnerable and was finding it increasingly difficult to lift her spirit.

She was looking at her whole life in a mirror; like an observer with a giant magnifying glass, focusing in on her own true self. Scrutinising every flaw and fault, bringing it all into the light. Grace had discovered that her life was a mirror, reflecting everything that was going on inside of her. There was no getting away from it, there was no out there, everything was coming from in here, within her.

Grace knew that she needed to make changes but she was clearly resisting, despite all of the signs that The Magician had been leaving for her. She preferred to blame everything on everyone else.

The journey was digging deep into her relationships too, for example her relationship with her mother for one. A mother she had no time for. Grace unconsciously blamed her for the split. She secretly wished that her father would come back. That everything would be okay, and they could be a happy family again, even after all these years. She resented her mother for not even trying to sort it all out in the early days. As a result, they tolerated each other, spending very little time together, and when they did, it was awkward and always ended in arguments.

But now in the clear light of day, Grace realised that her mother had done the best with what she had; struggling to bring Grace up alone and wrestling with her own personal demons at the same time. Grace had taken all of that for granted and had never really shown any level of empathy or appreciation. She couldn't even remember the last time she had told her mother that she loved her. In fact she couldn't even remember the last time she had seen her.

And love? What about love? Grace had two failed long term relationships. She had blamed it all on them and their inability to love her enough. She picked faults in each of them but really she was picking fault in herself. If truth be told she didn't love herself. So how on earth did she expect anyone else to truly love her? They couldn't. Protecting herself against future hurt, she wouldn't let them in. Grace's head was pounding. She knew all of this would have to be resolved, but she didn't know how.

CHAPTER 17

I AM

She barely made it to the bus stop on time and had no energy to speak to the driver.

When she eventually arrived at the old lady's house, she nearly collapsed through the doors. She was in a daze and couldn't even remember how she got there.

The old lady studied her. 'What's wrong with you dear? Are you coming down with something? You don't look yourself today, Grace. What can I get for you?'

'I'm not sure, I think I am just tired. I've not been feeling great recently and have been having a lot of bad dreams. They are keeping me awake and I just haven't been able to get a good night's sleep. I think everything is just catching up with me.'

'It doesn't surprise me at all. That's what happens when the body starts to detoxify. It's getting rid of all that rubbish you were storing up inside; all those negative thoughts, judgments and old memories. You are releasing all of the negative emotion and energy blocks from your system. This is a great sign, Grace. Well done. Keep up the good work!'

Grace looked at the old lady as if she was crazy. 'I am afraid it doesn't feel like that to me.'

'Listen to yourself, Grace. You are telling yourself you are afraid.'

'Afraid? What on earth are you talking about now?' Grace was getting really irritated by the conversation.

'I am not feeling well. Can't you see that? I am tired; in fact I am absolutely exhausted.' She was staring directly into the old woman's face.

'Now, now, Grace. What about all that love you learned about last week.' The old lady seemed to be finding a humorous side to all of this. Grace could not see anything funny about it at all.

'I am being serious, Grace. When you use the words **I Am** you are using the two most creative words in The Universe. When you use these two words, you give The Universe a message to create whatever it is you have attached to them, either positive or negative. These two words have an energy and power within them that can shape your reality.'

'When you say **I Am** afraid or **I Am** tired, you hold your energy in the vibration of fear and tiredness, and you simply cannot get well from that vibrational frequency.'

'Now let me see. Let's find a positive **I Am** to help you.' The old lady scurried across to her bookshelf and pulled out a book with a yellow cover and a big red love heart on the front. She opened it up as if she knew exactly the page she was looking for.

'Here we go…. repeat after me. 'I love and approve of myself. **I Am** completely at peace with the process of life.'

'What? This is ridiculous. How can that help me? Haven't you been listening? Don't you realise, I have spent the last week opening up wounds that I had buried away for years and all you can do to help is tell me to repeat some meaningless words?' Grace was now really angry and shouting at the old lady.

Unruffled the old lady grabbed Grace and hugged her close to her chest. As they met Grace felt a surge of warmth surround her heart. She began to shake.

'There, there Grace. That's okay. We still have to release some negative emotions and energy. Now breathe in and let it all go. Repeat after me; I love and approve of myself. **I Am** completely at peace with the process of life.'

Reluctantly, Grace began to say the words as she had been told.

'I love and approve of myself. **I Am** completely at peace with the process of life.'

She took a deep breath and repeated the words again as she exhaled 'I love and approve of myself. **I Am** completely at peace with the process of life.'

She repeated them several times and as she did so, she noticed her breathing was calming and her anger was dissolving.

'Can you feel it work, Grace?'

'Yes, I can actually' Grace found herself admitting in surprise.

'Great stuff. Now, all you have to do is keep repeating it. Eventually your body will create a new vibration and you will become well again and comfortable with all of the changes you are experiencing.'

'Come on, let's have some tea.' And they both moved towards the table and sat down.

'Vulnerability can be scary, Grace, but it is also the key to joy and happiness. And there is always Love – now you understand its power. It is deep within you. It is you. You are love. Enjoy it and embrace it. Grow in its power, feel it nurture you. You now understand that love is far more powerful than fear. Love will expose and dissolve your fears. Love will bring light to the darkness. But you have to accept and receive your gift of love. Accept and know you are worthy of love.'

'Does it make sense to you now? Do you remember what the books told you?' the old lady asked.

Grace looked at her and said 'Yes. It all makes perfect sense now. I remember. I am so sorry for shouting earlier. I didn't mean to...' Grace's overwhelming sense of remorse then quickly changed to gratitude as she leaned across to the old lady and gave her a huge heart-to-heart hug.

The old lady smiled. 'See, that feels good, doesn't it? I was a bit worried about you earlier. I knew you'd be okay though; there's an inner strength and resolve in there Grace' she said, pointing with her little finger towards Grace's heart. You are okay now aren't you?'

'Yes, **I Am**.'

CHAPTER 18

LADY DEATH

R ight, there's more to be done.' And forgetting about the tea she had promised, the old lady jumped up out of her seat and dropped to her knees on the floor. She lifted a tartan rug to reveal floorboards and what looked like a trap door with a ring pull. The old lady twisted and turned. It seemed stuck.

'I haven't opened this for years' she said.

Eventually the door gave way and the old lady fell back onto the floor, with her legs flying up into the air. She laughed and Grace laughed too.

Grace could see lots of steps that spiraled down and down under the house. 'Come on, follow me' and the old lady disappeared. Grace followed immediately, lowering herself down and into the void.

The steps were old and didn't look particularly safe. Grace wondered how the old lady managed to get down so quickly; she was already at the bottom waiting for her!

Grace found herself in an underground basement. 'Can you guess where we're going now?' the old lady laughed, teasing her.

'I haven't got a clue. I couldn't even hazard a guess.'

The old lady led Grace into a tunnel lined with strings of twinkling fairy lights and shining lanterns. 'It's beautiful, isn't it? I haven't been here for such a long time' said the old lady.

They wandered silently down the tunnel. As they reached the end Grace could hear the gentle lapping of water and realised they were approaching a jetty. They stopped at the edge and the old lady tugged on a rope and began to pull. Grace could see a small boat appear from the mist. The old lady pulled it to the side of the pier and said to Grace, 'In you go.'

Grace stepped cautiously into the boat as the old lady held it tight to the side. Once in, she took Grace's hand and, looking directly into her eyes, said 'It's going to be okay. Remember, forgiveness is the key' And with that the old lady seemed to vanish into thin air. She was getting good at that.

'Where are you?' Grace called out nervously as the boat began to drift away from the jetty. Grace could hear the water lap against the side of the tiny vessel. It was only then that she realised she was not alone. A dark, shadowy figure in a cloak sat in front of her. The figure was faceless.

Terrified, Grace asked 'Who are you? What do you want?'

Silence.

'Do you hear me? I asked, who are you?' Grace demanded.

The figure reached out but Grace recoiled. Then it spoke. 'Don't be afraid. I am Death, but you need not fear me.'

Although subconsciously Grace was surprised by the gentleness of the voice, fear gripped her and took over her thoughts.

She began to scream. 'Death? I'm dead? But I don't want to die. Not yet. I'm not ready.' Frightened and full of panic she continued to scream 'Please, I don't want to die. Please leave me alone, I'll be good. Someone save me.'

Death showed no emotion. None.

Grace crouched down and curled up into a little foetal ball on the floor of the boat, as far away from Death as she could get. She put her hands and arms tightly over her head like a child and tried to hide. She began to sob and as her body heaved, she whispered through her tears, 'I'm not ready to die. There are so many people I love, I need to tell them. I can't go now.'

The voice said 'Grace, listen to me. Death doesn't always mean what you think. You need to allow your old self to die to create a new life. Think about the two women at the lake, or the butterfly that emerged from the jar. A new life is being presented to you. You have to say goodbye to your old life. You have to let go. I know this is painful for you. I can feel it.'

'A death of sorts is necessary. I have come to show you the way. You do not need to fear me. I am here to help you.'

The shadowy figure stood over her and as Grace peered from beneath her arm Death stretched down and took hold of her right hand.

Grace kept her eyes closed tightly as Death squeezed her hand securely. Then the voice said 'Grace, let go. Forgive yourself and others. Set yourself free.'

'It's you that's holding me' Grace responded in a shaky voice. But as she tried to let go Grace realised it was she herself who was holding on to Death.

'Grace, it is you who is resisting. You are clinging on to your past. You think that it's safe because it is familiar. I am here to tell you that is not true. Grace, let go. Forgiveness is the key.'

Grace took a deep breath and from somewhere deep inside found the courage to let go of Death's hand. In that very moment her mind became completely quiet and still. No chatter in her head. Just complete silence. It was the oddest feeling and then it was gone. But it left behind absolute clarity.

She opened her eyes and looked up. She saw what looked to be a tornado spiral above her head. Looking closer she could see images, faces, events, words and people that had caused her pain in her past, and faces of those that she herself may have hurt in some way. They were flying around at light speed inside the whirlpool vortex.

As if directed by some invisible prompt Grace heard herself say, 'I forgive. **I Am** forgiven.'

As the words left her mouth, she was immediately thrown backwards into the boat by an extraordinarily powerful force of energy. There was a sudden explosion of light, and the images and faces shot straight up and through the centre of the tornado, disappearing into a black void at the top. Grace collapsed, gasping for air.

She lay quietly for a long while. When she eventually opened her eyes, Death had gone and in her place was the old lady. Grace jumped up, threw her arms around her neck and held on tight. 'You're not Death? You're not Death?'

The old lady pulled away from her slightly, looked into her hazel eyes, smiled and said, 'No, I am not Death Grace, but I have seen Death on a few occasions. I thought you should meet her. It was time. You were ready.'

CHAPTER 19

SCIENCE AND SPACE

Springing out of bed and hardly able to contain herself, Grace felt a real optimism about her future. It made her want to sing and dance all day long.

Work colleagues continued to comment and other people had noticed it too. Everyone was looking at her strangely. How bizarre to think that people consider you odd for being happy, she thought and began to laugh.

She reflected on all of the events she had experienced during her visits with the old lady. How could she possibly discuss this with anyone? They would think she was mad or delusional! And yet to her it felt very real. Grace felt completely liberated and it was so invigorating. Her thoughts had changed and her emotions were different, in fact she felt like a completely different human being.

She caught her usual bus. Grace now preferred this mode of travel to her car. It was much more interesting listening to the driver and his stories. When she arrived at the house, the old lady opened the patio doors anticipating Grace's arrival.

Grace jumped back, startled. 'Oh my goodness' she said, 'Now what?'

The old lady was dressed like a whacky pilot. She wore tight gold trousers and a bomber jacket in her signature tartan. She was also sporting a gold helmet and huge flying goggles. Grace stared in astonishment.

'What's wrong with you?'

'Nothing' said Grace 'I'm just fascinated by your outfit!'

The old lady laughed, 'Oh, this old thing, I've had it for years, and there's a reason why I'm dressed like this, we're going somewhere unusual today.'

'Oh. Where's that then?' asked Grace as she raised an eyebrow quizzically.

'Space' the old lady said. Grace burst out laughing.

'I'm serious. Now that you have sorted yourself out and released everything that has been holding you back, I thought it was time for you to see the bigger picture. It's time to see the world from a whole new perspective.'

'Let's go' and with that she took Grace's hand and led her towards a wooded area behind the house. There was a narrow path which led to a set of steps winding up beyond a mass of shrubs and bushes before disappearing beneath the foliage.

'You're going to love this' the old lady exclaimed as they both started up the steps. Grace was amazed at how quickly the old lady moved. It was as if she had springs on her boots. Grace struggled to keep up with her.

Up and up they went until they arrived at a small clearing, and there right in the centre, stood an old wooden shed.
'Here we are' the old lady said proudly, 'This is it.'

'We have come all the way up here for this?' said Grace, clearly disappointed.

Sensing Grace's mood the old lady said 'Oh, don't worry, remember nothing is ever as it seems' and gave her a cheeky wink.

Grace shook her head, 'Okay.'

The door to the hut was hanging limply on one hinge. There may as well not have been any door there at all. As they manoeuvered past, into the body of the shed, Grace was staggered by what she saw. Even by the old lady's standards this was unbelievable. Right in front of her was a spaceship! Gunmetal grey and circular, with a huge panoramic window that wrapped all the way around.

'What is that?' Grace asked, astounded.

'It's my spaceship of course. Doesn't everyone have one?' The old lady laughed with that infectious chortle of hers. 'I haven't been up here for ages. Oh, how I've missed him' she said, as she lovingly patted the steely exterior.

'Now where is it ...?' The old lady muttered to herself as she walked purposefully towards a dusty wardrobe at the back of the shed. Its rickety doors looked as if they were about to fall off too.

The old lady disappeared inside the wardrobe, and as she did, began to throw things up into the air and out onto the floor behind her. Old bits of spaceship, spanners, tools, springs, a can of oil, balls of string, a yellow watering can and a pair of tartan wellies went flying through the air, creating a massive dust cloud in their wake.

Grace stood still and watched.

Finally, the old lady said 'Ahh … here it is' and she emerged waving a silver helmet above her dusty white hair before handing it to Grace. 'Here, put this on.' She looked comical with her face covered in thick soot. Grace bit her lip and tried hard to contain her laughter.

'Ehh, what for?' she asked the old lady.

'I told you we are going on a long journey, and oh boy are you going to need it! And Grace, you're going to need these too!' the old lady giggled as she handed Grace a pink leather biker jacket and matching goggles.

Grace was getting more confused by the minute. 'Remind me where we are going again?' she asked as she started to remove her own jacket in order to try on the pink one. She rather liked it, and it fitted her perfectly.

'Space, I told you!' said the old lady.

Grace raised her eyebrows and thought she would just humour her. 'Okay, so how do we get there?' she said.

'How do you think? In this of course!' the old lady said, as she caressed the side of the spaceship.

Grace almost choked. 'No chance! You're not going to get me in that!'

'Listen, it's perfectly safe. The last time I was up in here….eh' and the old lady looked upward searching for a date, 'Yes, it must be over twenty years now. Goodness is it that long?' she said as she scratched her head in amazement. 'Well anyway, he flew like a dream back then. So there is absolutely nothing to worry about.'

Nothing about this conversation was reassuring Grace in the slightest.

The old lady stopped and looked at her, and this time she was serious.

'Look, I promise you it will be fine. I wouldn't put you in any danger. You have to trust me. And aren't you just a little bit curious?'

Grace was curious alright. But if she was being entirely honest with herself she was also worried that she was going to die in a tiny machine somewhere in space with no-one able to find her ….,ever.

Grace caught herself thinking. Space? …of course we're not going to space … this is just ridiculous!

'Oh, you need to put these on too' chuckled the old lady as she handed Grace the tartan wellies which matched the old lady's jacket.

Okay, I'll just go with this and see what happens thought Grace. Nothing else for it.

She pulled on the goggles and then the helmet. She laughed at how silly she must be looking standing in this ransack of a barn dressed like a misfit from outer space.

There's still time to say no, thought Grace as she stood staring at the spaceship. She was immediately transported back to her childhood, standing at the top of a super slide at a water park. That point where you say *okay I will* and then just as quickly change your mind and think *oh no, I can't.*

Grace certainly did not want that awful feeling where you slink back down the stairs, on an embarrassing walk of shame, against a flurry of people going in the opposite direction. She remembered the little magician boy and his talk about overcoming fear. Seconds later she zipped up her jacket resolutely and walked confidently over to the spaceship.

Meanwhile, the old lady was checking something on the undercarriage of the craft.

'Can I help with anything?' Grace offered.

'No, we're all good to go! Let's climb aboard' and she directed Grace up the ladder and into the hatch.

Once inside, Grace was surprised to find that the spaceship's interior was a lot more spacious than it looked from the outside; not quite tardis-like but surprisingly roomy all the same, equipped with all the necessary requisites for space-age travel. Two seats sat side-by-side at the front of the craft. There were gadgets, gizmos, lights and fancy electronics. The 360° window, like a gigantic fish bowl, magnified everything outside. Grace could see little sleeping pods nestling at the rear of the cabin. This was really cool thought Grace.

'Where should I sit?' she asked. For the first time she realised she was extremely excited.

'Here, the seat marked "co-pilot." I might need your help; it's been a while since I've flown' said the old lady with a giggle.

Grace gulped, 'You're not expecting me to fly this thing? I've never flown or done anything like this before.'

'Don't worry. I'm sure I'll remember as I go along. Just sit down and enjoy the view.'

Grace sat down and hastily strapped herself in. There was a plaque fixed in the middle of the dials and Grace leaned forward to read it.

"We are all visitors to this time, this place. We are just passing through. Our purpose here is to observe, to learn, to grow, to love ... and then we return home."

The old lady settled down beside her and followed her gaze. 'Yes, that's lovely isn't it? I had almost forgotten that it was there. Inspired words indeed.'

She then slapped the dashboard as if she was telling Grace to do an emergency stop in her driving test and said 'Here, you must be impressed with all these gadgets and gizmos, Grace?' motioning to the vast array of lights on the panel in front of her.

'Yes, I am, although there are so many. It must be really difficult to fly this plane or spaceship or whatever ...' and Grace's voice trailed off.

'Ha-ha, not really, it's an automatic' the old lady laughed, as she pressed a large green button marked GO.

Grace could feel the spacecraft stirring and coming to life. There was a steady pulse, a gently building vibration, and then the comforting sound of everything clicking into gear, preparing for lift off.

The old lady closed her eyes 'What a fantastic piece of engineering this is. Can you feel how in tune it is?'

'Yes, oddly I can' said Grace, and she meant it.

'Right, 5,4,3,2,1, we're off!' said the old lady. Grace joined in by letting out an excited 'Woo-hoo!'

The spaceship started to lurch forward, a bit shaky at first, as if waking up and stretching after a long slumber. It started edging slowly towards the shed door. Grace hid behind her fingers as she realised that the spaceship wasn't stopping and was going right through it.

'Ah, don't worry, I'll get that replaced once we get back' said the old lady, quite unconcerned.

Suddenly they were outside in the brilliant bright sunshine. The spaceship gathered momentum. It was evidently excited by its first venture outside for years. It felt like an eager puppy straining on a leash to get to the next corner.

'Whoa there! Calm down, take it easy!' instructed the old lady as if the spaceship could hear her.

The spaceship shot right off the edge of the hill and over some tree tops. Grace felt her stomach somersault. She thought they would crash but instead the spaceship shot straight up vertically into the air, rising faster and faster. Everything became a massive blur and Grace couldn't see anything at all except streaks of coloured light that zoomed past her head. She could feel the skin on her face getting pulled back, tighter and tighter, like a magic facelift.

Up and up and up they went. She had no idea for how long.

Then unexpectedly everything stopped. Complete darkness. The spaceship leveled off. It was as if they were now sitting suspended somewhere in a black hole. Lights flickered on the dashboard and they were bathed in a pale fluorescent glow. Grace caught her breath and looked over at the old lady. She was calmly removing her helmet and smoothing down her grey hair, which, due to the static, was completely wild and sticking out all over the place. Grace could hear the old lady's hair crackling with electricity.

Grace removed her own helmet and realised that her hair was also standing on end. She laughed at her reflection in the window.

'Where are we? And why is it so dark? I can't see anything.'

'You'll see soon enough. Be patient' said the old lady.

Grace sat silently. She waited and watched. She was alive with anticipation and the excitement of the unknown.

Slowly an infinite universe of stars began to emerge. It was incredibly beautiful and moving. One by one little twinkling lights appeared until they became one swirling mass of white stars, one hundred billion galaxies wide.

Grace knew that the stars were positioned at varying distances and light years away from her. It was as if she was at the centre of a 4D Milky Way hologram. She struggled to assimilate the experience. It was utterly majestic, beyond words.

'Do you notice the spiraling and shell-like shapes of space?'

'Yes. I do.' Grace said, as she suddenly became aware of the never ending whirlpool designs of the solar system and star constellations.

The old lady whispered. 'Grace, "The One" who created The Universe, loves circles.'

And with that she reached down and pressed a blue button marked Warp Drive and tearing through stars and galaxies, they were instantly propelled 7,000 light years into space.

They stopped amidst what looked like a colossal cloud formation of finger like protrusions of blues, browns and yellows. A sunburst had exploded behind the outer edges of the clouds, outlining each one in radiant silver. Stars twinkled in a hazy turquoise blue backdrop. The great Masters could not have painted a more inspiring scene.

'Where are we? What is this?' Grace was virtually speechless. She rubbed her eyes several times to make sure this vision in front of her was real.

'This is known as "The Pillars of Creation", Grace. It is a nebulous cloud at the heart of space itself. Within these explosions of gas and dust, new stars are being birthed into existence.'

Grace was in awe. Her senses were exploding. Every cell in her body became alive and in harmony with the vastness of this eternal solar system which enfolded her. She was conscious, and space was conscious too! It was not the emptiness and nothingness that she had always believed.

As her eyes filled with tears, the droplets flicked off her face floating upwards in perfect little orbs. She felt a consciousness, connection and belonging that she had never known before.

The old lady was looking at her and Grace sensed she was experiencing it too. They smiled at each other knowingly, and then sat for what seemed like eternity as two humble and privileged observers of this supernatural wonder.

Eventually the old lady broke the silence. 'Let's take a closer look at our little planet, Grace' and she manoeuvered the vessel around and towards home.

Travelling through space and time at warp speed Grace could only marvel at the scale, beauty and drama of it. It was too much for her to process intellectually and emotionally. She had a million questions about how and why and what. Her head was whirling, spinning.

As they progressed homewards Grace let out a gasp when she saw Earth as a planet for the first time. It was a profound moment as she viewed her world from a completely new and expanded perspective.

She saw Earth as a giant spaceship which traversed The Universe just like the Moon, or Saturn or Venus. It looked so magnificent yet so fragile, just hanging there. She could see her planet as blues and greens and whites, dynamic and alive. A giant blue marble teeming with diversity and rolling its way around the sun to sustain life. It was breathtaking.

'Where are your goggles, Grace?'

'Right here' she replied.

'These goggles turn the invisible into visible.'

'Really?' Grace was now so used to the impossible becoming possible that she barely reacted to the old lady's statement.

'Yes they do. There is a dial around the rim of the right goggle. Can you see it?'

'Yes, I can.'

'Turn it anti-clockwise between the IR and UV setting, please.'
'Okay, done' Grace announced.

'You see, Grace, our Universe is more invisible than visible. Just because we can't see something, doesn't mean it's not there. That is the mistake the majority of people make. Your relationship with the invisible is what will ultimately define your life.'

She continued, 'Our human eyes can only detect a microcosm of the huge spectrum of what actually exists. These goggles allow us to extend that range way out past the normal visible colours of the rainbow, to detect infra-red, ultra violet, microwave and radio waves. These all exist in our Universe and contain vital information that we can't normally pick up with our limited human senses. But these goggles will!'

'Pop them on, Grace and let's take a look. Don't you just love the science?' and then she laughed.

Grace stretched the elastic over her head and positioned the goggles carefully around her eyes. As she began to focus on Earth, the blues and greens changed into swirls of deep reds and oranges and yellows.

'That's the heat from the Earth you are seeing, Grace. It's the planet reacting to sunlight, absorbing and reflecting the radiation coming from our local star, the sun, 93 million miles away!'

Grace was mesmerised. She had only ever seen things like this in *National Geographic* and now she was actually part of it.

'Now, to show you the next thing, I need to turn the Earth upside down or should I say turn us upside down!' and at that she pushed the warp drive button again, and in seconds they were half way around the planet to its most southerly point.

Grace saw a huge white land mass. She detected no red nor orange light, only a cold steely blue radiating upwards towards her. She shivered looking at it.

'That's Antarctica. It receives very little of the sun's energy, and what it does receive, it reflects back out into space. It's frozen and plunged in darkness for almost six months of the year. Temperatures are minus one hundred degrees Fahrenheit and it has winds that rage constantly at over one hundred miles an hour. But this icy continent sustains tropical rainforests 5,000 miles away in the Amazon. You see, Grace, everything is connected. Change your goggles to R and we will pick up radio wave signals.' Grace did as she was told and she refocused her lenses.

Suddenly everything was '3D'.

'Now look here' and the old lady pointed below.

As Grace followed the old lady's finger, she could see what looked like a 3D map of the ocean floor. An enormous blue underwater river was flowing through vast chasms miles deep in the sea bed, merging with submarine waterfalls that plummeted into the dark abyss of the Earth's crust.

'That's the great Ocean Conveyor. It's caused by the salty water driven up from Antarctica. What goes on there affects the whole planet.'

Grace found all of this totally fascinating, she was learning so much and learning fast from her teacher.

'Turn your goggles to M and let's get a microwave picture of a storm at sea. The old lady was really excited as she pointed out and into the vast ocean.

This time Grace could see millions of tons of water vapour; huge seas warmed by the sun, condensing into cloud systems which reached ten miles high. As the Earth rotated these were spun into a vast vortex of thunder clouds which looked oddly similar to some of the whirling galaxies she had just observed above.

'Grace, you are witnessing the birth of a hurricane. I think that this one will blow off before it reaches land' the old lady said reassuringly.

Turning her goggles back to visible range, Grace saw a massive bloom of green spread along the edges of China. 'That's phytoplankton. They are the tiny organisms that produce at least half of the oxygen we breathe and they also provide a feeding frenzy for marine life. Everything, no matter how small, has a crucial role to play in the grand scheme of things. Everything is necessary for the whole to function. Everything is interdependent.'

Grace's view then travelled from China to Africa where she saw the sand storms of the Sahara Desert and winds blow mineral enriched sand-dust across the Atlantic to South America, where they fertilised the rain forests of the Amazon. Yes, it is true, she realised, everything is connected.

From this orbit she could see the whole planet. Electrical storms raged far beneath her, creating lightning flashes a thousand miles apart which seemed to set each other off like fireworks. It reminded her of the Van de Graff generator experiments she loved in her physics classroom, only way bigger.

Grace sat back in her co-pilot seat and removed her goggles. She was looking at the story of the planet's ecosystem; an intricately interwoven web of life. Grace felt so grateful to have experienced this precious view of our world.

'Thank you for sharing this with me' she said.

'You are very welcome, my dear' the old lady responded.

'Grace, tell me what does all of this mean to you? What do you see?'

'It's funny, I think I am more aware of what I don't see right now. Up here I don't see governments or industries or businesses. I don't see streets or houses or individual people. I don't see challenges or the stresses of day-to-day living. This picture seems so much bigger and much more important. Does that make sense?' she asked the old lady.

'Yes of course it does, Grace. I am so pleased that you have this new level of awareness.'

Grace continued, 'But what I do see is nature being exactly what it should be despite our intervention, operating effortlessly and perfectly. I see a world where everything is connected and a part of the whole. The whole of space. The Universe.'

Pausing for a moment and looking out into infinity, Grace said quietly, 'But I also feel sadness in my heart, knowing how privileged I am to see this magnificent overview of Earth and I wonder, if everyone could see things from this vantage point, would life on Earth be different? Better?'

'Yes, Grace that is a very important question. Perhaps if everyone could see from this perspective, they would treat our home with the care and reverence of a steward.'

And with that thought ricocheting through Grace's mind, the old lady pushed the throttle forward.

CHAPTER 20

INNER SPACE

Before we get into the detail, I want to show you something quite remarkable.' The old lady pointed to the south and north poles. 'Can you see the dazzling and colourful dance of the Aurora, Grace?'

'Yes. It's stunning. I've always wondered how that happens.'

'You have just seen the incredible life giving energy of the sun and its effect on our planet. Yes?' she asked rhetorically.

'Well, the sun also has the potential to wreak havoc on our little planet. Every second it is emitting dangerous bursts of super-heated, charged particles. Billions of them are hurtling towards us right now at a million miles per hour!'

Grace grimaced and looked terrified.

'Without some kind of protection these enormous blasts would strip away our atmosphere, destroy our eco system and scorch us. And if that's not enough they would dry up our oceans and leave behind a planet as barren and bleak as Mars!'

'What a terrible thought.' Grace recoiled at this idea and the appalling image of a dead and red burnt Earth.

'I know. It's not a great thought is it?' The old lady made a silly face and shrugged her shoulders.

'But fortunately for us' she announced with great gusto 'the Earth has an invisible shield; a magical magnetic force field called the magnetosphere. It protects us from that potentially devastating outcome. It works with the Earth's inner magnetic fields and steers the radioactive particles down towards the polar regions.'

'This is an extremely energetic process and as the radiation circles the poles, it excites the air molecules in the atmosphere and triggers something we can see with our very own eyes. One of nature's true wonders, the northern and southern lights or the Aurora Borealis and the Aurora Australis.'

'It's phenomenal' said Grace in a hushed tone. 'It's like a glorious crown of the most beautiful greens, purples, pinks and violets. But thank goodness for our invisible power shield.' Grace drew a breath of relief.

'How do you know so much about all of this? And how do you remember all of it?' she asked the old lady.

'I am really not sure. My brain just seems to absorb vast amounts of interconnected information and pieces it all together making complex subjects a little easier for people to understand.'

'At school they use to call me "Mesmo, the Memory Man" and she laughed at the fond memory. 'I am told the correct name for it today is a Synthesizer!'

'Anyway, that's not really why I am showing you all of this. Pop your goggles on and turn the dial to EMF which stands for Electro Magnetic Field and I'll show you what I really wanted you to see!'

Grace was a little confused but did exactly what she was told. The old lady asked her to take her gaze just above the Earth. 'Can you see it, Grace?'

'What?'

'Look outside and around the Earth's stratosphere? Can you see anything?'

'Yes, I think I can.' Grace then proceeded to describe what she saw. 'I see faint circular waves coming out of the Earth at the north and south poles. They are mushrooming out and circling the Earth like a giant donut of energy.'

'Perfect description. Yes that's exactly right. That's the Earth's Electro Magnetic Field. Now remember that shape, Grace. You are going to see it somewhere else later.'

Grace was curious. 'Okay. That's enough of outer space let's take this baby to inner space!' and with that the old lady pressed a yellow button on the control panel marked Quantum.

The spaceship shot straight down on an apparent collision course with Earth but stopped conveniently in a large hole in the ozone layer.

'Grace, look here. Can you see and feel those dark lesions across the planet?' The old lady began to point out grey shadows all across the globe. 'Now tune in. What do you feel?'

Grace closed her eyes and imagined the dark blots in her mind. Instantly she experienced intense heat and an excruciating pain shot right through her body. It made her convulse. 'What was that?' she yelped.

'Those are war scars in the Earth's "skin", the legacy of centuries of war and conflict. They leave footprints, negative hotspots; energetic reminders of the hate and fear that caused them.'

'That's dreadful' said Grace.

'If you think that's bad just look at these.' And the old lady began to point out luminous abrasions on the planet's surface. They were emitting dense and ominous vibrations and were clustered in various locations across the world. Some in Russia, others along the West Coast of America and the Pacific Ocean. Two in Japan and the rest dotted about randomly.

'Oooh, they feel awful. What are they?' Grace felt physically sick from tuning into this energy.

'It's nuclear radiation, Grace. What you are seeing and feeling is the residual energy of the bombings, incidents and the thousands of nuclear tests that have occurred in the last century. Can you imagine what that has done to our fragile eco system?'

Grace was shocked at this revelation. 'I didn't know.'

'And you're not alone, Grace. There is so much more happening to our world that is not common knowledge. Intervention, manipulation and unquestioned intrusion into the very identity of our planet, plant, animal and human species. Secret, invisible, destruction.'

Grace could not believe what she was hearing. 'Why did I not know this?'

'Because like most people Grace, you were asleep. But you are awake now.'

'Okay. That's enough of that. I can feel the energy too.' The old lady was clearly angry.

Grace looked at her. She had never seen her like this before, like a mother protecting her child.

The old lady hit the Quantum button again and they immediately shot right through the atmosphere, over continents and countries. Down, down, down, settling above a highly populated city.

'Where are we now?' Grace sounded nervous, her voice faltering. She was just a little concerned that they would be observed by military radar and shot down as a suspected UFO!

'Don't worry' said the old lady. 'I have activated our invisibility shield. No one can see or detect us. All is well.'

Of course we have an invisibility shield thought Grace, how complacent of me to think otherwise. She was no longer one bit surprised by anything the old lady said or did. Reassured, she asked 'What city is it?'

'It doesn't really matter. What you are going to experience here is universal. You will find it in every city, town and person on the planet. Pop your goggles back on and turn them to Universal. It's a really sensitive mode. You will pick up all the finer energies and human emotional vibrations and frequencies. I think that you'll find this really interesting.'

As Grace peered through the craft's magnified bubble window she saw people scurrying about on the streets below, oblivious to the world around them, and to the invisible spaceship hovering above them. But it wasn't the individuals or their behavior that interested her. It was their energy. It was visible and she could feel it!

Everyone appeared mostly shades of grey, their energy felt dense.

Grace adjusted her goggles and was astonished to realise that she could now see right through buildings and into office spaces. It was as if Grace had just put on a pair of x-ray glasses.

'Wow. This is nuts' said Grace. 'I can see right through walls.'

In the offices people by and large looked either stressed or bored; they also looked dull and grey, she could feel their low vibration. Something caught Grace's eye. She saw a figure in one of the office blocks, it moved from floor to floor, chatting, smiling, saying hello and just generally being pleasant. Grace saw and felt a very different energy emanating from this person. It flowed from their heart; it felt warm and glowed green like a fiery emerald. The iridescent figure belonged to the office tea lady. With a knowing smile, the old lady turned the spacecraft around and forward.

Moments later Grace found herself hovering above the local park. They zoomed in on a father and son sitting on a park bench. Although everything around them was monochrome she observed the same green glow pulsate from their chests.

They were chatting and the father was looking up into the sky and pointing. Grace hoped it wasn't at her! As he pointed things out, the young boy laughed and looked excited. The glowing green energy between them intensified and expanded way, way out; at least eight feet beyond their physical bodies. The energy also seemed to ebb and flow in waves between them like a gentle green tide. She could see a visible energy loop, circle from their heads to their hearts and link together.

Grace could feel their energy too. It felt like she was absorbing waves of love. 'What is that I am seeing and feeling?' she said as she turned to the old lady for an explanation.

'It's called "Coherence", Grace. When two people are totally in sync with each other and with their environment, particularly when they are experiencing an expression of love, then their physical, mental and emotional energy systems are coherent. Isn't it wonderful? It's the optimum energy. Miracles happen when we are in this state of being. If everyone lived in coherence, there would be no wars, no conflict, and no inequality. We would truly experience global peace.'

Grace felt peace settle in her heart.

'I think this is a great place to take you quantum again' and before Grace could say a word the old lady hit the Quantum button.

But this time something very different happened. The spaceship began to shake uncontrollably and the walls began to press in towards them. As Grace looked out of the window she was shocked to see the park grow in size. She was shrinking! Outside grew bigger and bigger and inside grew smaller and smaller.

'Agghhhh!' she screamed, knowing exactly how Alice felt in her strange Wonderland. 'What's happening? I am going to disappear!' she screamed hysterically.

'Oh! Shush, Grace. You're such a big scaredy cat!' the old lady was laughing unperturbed. She then looked directly at Grace and said in a calming voice 'Honey, I've shrunk the spaceship!' breaking the moment with uncontrollable laughter.

'You've done what?' but before she got an answer the spaceship shot forward heading straight for the father's heart!'

'We're going to kill him.' Grace screamed and squeezed her eyes shut tightly as the spacecraft entered the man's body through his white shirt, just managing to avoid a collision with a gigantic button.

'No we're not. We are too small' replied the old lady.

'We are too what? What are you saying?' Grace was in shock.

'I am telling you we are the size of an atom, Grace. He won't feel a thing. I promise.'

And with that Grace fainted.

When she regained consciousness, she was completely disorientated. 'Where am I? What happened?'

The old lady pressed a cold cloth against her forehead. 'You're fine, pet. You just got a bit of a shock, that's all.'

'Yes, I was dreaming I was inside a human body. It was terrifying' Grace whispered.

'It isn't a dream, Grace; we are inside a human body. Quite near the heart actually!'

Grace sat bolt upright and looked around. As she stared in disbelief through the 360° window, she saw a gigantic red throbbing muscle. It was a heart! She closed her eyes and then opened them again, but it was still there. She could see tiny veins on its surface and blood move continuously and effortlessly through them. 'What's that noise?' Grace became aware of a slow regular and rhythmic drum noise.

'Oh that's his heartbeat. It would appear we didn't kill him after all!' The old lady tried to smile but could see it was not perhaps entirely appropriate based on how Grace was looking at her. Changing the subject she said 'Okay. Now that you've composed yourself, pop your goggles on and let's have a look at this through the EMF spectrum.'

Grace was still shaking but reluctantly put on the goggles and re-adjusted her focus. She didn't know what to expect or see next. As she turned her attention to the man's heart, Grace observed faint circular waves emanating from the top and the bottom of the heart muscle. They then mushroomed out and circled the heart like a giant donut of energy.

The old lady was staring at her.

Grace immediately saw the connection and turned to look at the old lady in amazement.

'Yes I told you that you would see this shape again. Didn't I?' It was the exact same Electro Magnetic Field that Grace had seen earlier protecting the planet from the sun.

'This is a miracle' said Grace.

'I suppose it is, Grace. Life is a miracle' agreed the old lady.

'The heart is the electromagnetic power house of our body, our Universe. It is way more powerful than the brain and directs and orchestrates everything in our life effortlessly and miraculously, if we allow it! Its energy can be picked up eight to ten feet outside of our bodies. You saw that, didn't you, in the park when you were watching the man and his son lovingly interact.'

The old lady became philosophical. 'As above, so below. As without, so within. The macrocosm and the microcosm are connected.'

Staring at Grace intently she asked, 'You don't actually believe that we are separate or different from our Universe, do you? Surely not? Not now?' The old lady then looked directly into her eyes and said gently 'Grace, we **are** The Universe.'

This was way too much for Grace to absorb.

'Let me show you a couple of other things that might help you understand Grace.' And she pressed Quantum again.

This time they followed a multitude of tiny red blood cells swimming in and out of a myriad of chambers and tunnels throughout the body. Grace soon realised they were travelling inside the man's veins.

The cells seemed to be working away relentlessly, carrying oxygen and nourishing every part of the body. Grace could see body parts come to life, re-energised and revitalised as these little cells removed dangerous carbon dioxide and replaced it with life-giving pure, clean oxygen.

'I love these guys' Grace said as she watched the little 'body helpers' do their vital work.

'Yes, I do too. They are so selfless. They are completely content to carry out the same function and task, day in day out. They never tire or get bored. Do you know why, Grace?' And instantly the old lady answered herself with one word, "Purpose!" They understand their individual purpose, and their purpose as part of the whole.'

Grace sat quietly, absorbing it all.

'Take a closer look at them, Grace. Do you notice anything?'

As Grace began to scrutinise the tiny blood cells she noticed something embedded in nearly every single one of them. It looked like a tiny map of a human body. But how could this be and what did it mean? Grace was perplexed.

She looked at the old lady for help. 'Yes, Grace. What you are seeing is absolutely true. Within nearly every living cell of the body there is a blue print of the whole. Each cell, in addition to its individual and distinct purpose, also contains the entire genetic code of the whole body.'

'That's why they perform at their best, always. They know their purpose and its importance in sustaining life. It's a miracle indeed.'

Grace was totally overwhelmed with this thought. She recalled how she moaned about her job, rather than appreciating it and her contribution to her clients' well-being. She felt momentarily ashamed.

'Okay, one last thing Grace before we leave this lovely man alone. This will totally explode every synapse in your brain, so be prepared!'

Grace wasn't sure what that meant, but she was sure she was about to see something monumental.

'Sit down and buckle yourself in for this, Grace. Oh, and I would put your helmet on too.'

Grace obeyed immediately. The old lady looked down at the last remaining button on her controls. It was iridescent purple and it read Quantum Jump. As the old lady pressed the button Grace experienced the very same feeling that she had when travelling through space at light speed. Faster and faster they went and then everything just stopped. Complete darkness. Once again, Grace felt as if they were suspended somewhere in a big black hole. Lights flickered on the dashboard and they were bathed in the same pale fluorescent glow.

Grace caught her breath. 'This is like Déjà Vu' and she looked over at the old lady.

'Yes, it is rather' the old lady laughed.

'Look out of the window, Grace.'

Grace followed her direction and walked over to the craft's enormous convex window. She pressed her face against it. Slowly, an infinite universe began to emerge from the darkness. A universe of lights that one minute appeared here, and the next minute, appeared way over there. It was as if they were jumping. She saw a matrix of waves large and small everywhere and then nowhere at all. Everything was pulsing and flashing on and off.

'Where are we now?' she asked.

'We are in the weird quantum world of energy, Grace. We are right at the heart of the body's energy system. Although we look solid we are actually just a fluctuating entanglement of energy, infinite fractals of omnipotent consciousness.'

Grace wasn't listening. She had spotted something moving way out in the dark void. Intuitively she put on her goggles and turned them between the UV and MW setting. She wanted to pick up both the ultra violet and microwave spectrum for this.

Her vision became highly sensitive and she could see the vivid colours of the full spectrum. Everything was 4D.

Way out in this "inner space" she saw what looked like a tiny sun. Spinning around it were little planets, just like the Earth and the moon. In fact it could have been any of the planets in the solar system. Against this back drop of a miniscule, little galaxy of twinkling intermittent lights, she stood in silence and in awe and then turned to the old lady.

'It's an atom, Grace. At its centre is the nucleus and those are electrons and protons orbiting it. And yes, it does look like a tiny universe.' A tear dropped onto Grace's cheek.

The two women walked to meet each other and embraced. As they did so a faint tendril of green energy flowed from their hearts and mushroomed like a huge donut enfolding their bodies.

The old lady whispered in Grace's ear. 'Grace, when we hurt our world and our Universe we hurt ourselves. Because it is ourselves.'

'I know' said Grace in a quiet childlike voice. 'As above, so below. As without, so within.'

CHAPTER 21

GRACE

It was just about dawn. As Grace peered out of her bedroom window she could see dark purple clouds tinged with the orange of the rising sun scattered across the horizon. Only a sprinkling of the night's stars were left in the sky which was illuminated by a slice of silver moon.

She sat upright in bed, puffed up all four rose-patterned pillows and leaned back gazing into space. The beauty of what she was looking at had a completely new meaning to her. She revelled in the stillness of the moment.

Reaching across to her bedside cabinet she turned on the little Tiffany lamp, opened the drawer and picked up "The Book" that the tall man had given her. Looking at the cover, she announced 'Grace' to the empty room. She opened "The Book" at the first page and read the words, *It all starts with a blank page…a space to create.*

Grace thought about the amazing adventures that had taken place over the last few months. She began to review them individually in an attempt to piece everything together and make some sense of it all. Like a list of contents, she wrote a title for each of the "Chapters" as she called them. She then began to jot down little aide-memoires beside each one, detailing what had happened and what she had learned.

She recalled the odd situation of the wrong bus which had taken her to the beautiful Gothic church; the place where she was first magnetised and inextricably drawn to the old woman. She now realised that this was no coincidence and that their paths were destined to meet.

There was the surreal experience at the beginning of time on the beach, and the discovery of The Creation Process. She loved meeting the famous inventors and creatives who with their monumental vision and purpose had proven this timeless Creation theory.

She laughed as she remembered the funny tartan RESET button which had been so helpful when she needed to change her thought process, her mood or to see things more positively. The science of this was so interesting to her. Discovering that energy was like a wave with a frequency and that we could manage this energy to help us influence what we create. This was an inspiring awareness.

And then there was the series of the extraordinary women; The Spirit of Adventure, the young girl and her older self, the lady with the white sari and Lady Death; they had all brought her messages of love, compassion and forgiveness. Grace discovered how these powerful emotions help us live in our natural creative flow and achieve our heart's desire.

Not forgetting the little Magician Boy, who left messages for her everywhere "encouraging" her to be bold and make change.

Finally the macroscopic and microscopic universes which helped her understand that she was connected to, and at one with everything. That everything "out there" mirrored everything "in here."

There was no doubt that it had been an unbelievably extraordinary experience and with so much learning it was little wonder her mind was whizzing, spinning and somersaulting in every direction.

But these discoveries, however remarkable, were only half the story of her adventure. The other half was Grace's own personal journey. Up until now Grace had been asleep. Asleep to herself. Asleep to other people. Asleep to her world and to The Universe.

She began to scribble notes in "The Book."

I was exhausted with life. I was stressed and had no energy for anything other than work. I was caught on the treadmill and unable to jump off. I was completely disconnected from my community, my colleagues, my family, myself. I had no awareness at all that I may have been responsible for what was happening in my life or what I was creating.

I belonged to nothing and nowhere. Yet I longed to. I longed to know my purpose. My heart's desire. But I never knew that is what I longed for.

I was angry. Angry at them. But now I know that just hurt me. I forgave and I was forgiven.

I Am awake now. I believe the awakening began when I met her. She awakened me. She taught me what life was really about. She taught me about the creative power that is life. That is me. She taught me to see life through rose coloured glasses or "goggles" even!

Now I feel happy for no apparent reason, just like the old lady looked when I first met her. I Am energised, light and alive. I want to laugh and sing and dance all day long. I Am free.

For the first time in my life I know I belong. Not to a club, group, or a Facebook page; but to a Universe that is intelligent, alive and abundant. A Universe that I believe has my best interests at heart. I am connected to people, animals, plants and Mother Nature. I am part of a miraculous living breathing planet. I Am unique and I have a purpose. My life has meaning. I have something valuable to contribute. I Am a Creator.

Her pen flowed effortlessly with these words. Words that she could never have expressed before meeting the old lady. The words seemed to be writing themselves through her. It was as if she was simply an observer or a conduit for every word that seemingly wrote itself onto the page of "The Book."

Her thoughts shifted to the old lady; this beautiful, graceful, wise, quirky, dynamic little scientist. Grace truly loved her and she knew that the old lady loved her too. The old lady had taught her so much. But why? Why her? Why had the old lady chosen her? Why was she the recipient of such incredible knowledge and timeless wisdom?'

Grace was so grateful for her teacher and instinctively wrote a thankyou note in "The Book."

A whole hearted thankyou for being my inspired teacher. I Am infinitely grateful for you being in my life. I have learned so much. You told me I was ready and I was. Thank you for your guidance and insight. Thank you for showing me the way. I have such a clear sense of bigger things to come. Thank you. I love you.

It felt good to write it and as she did, the energy of appreciation amplified a million times. Gratitude shot through her body like an electrical current. She was amazed at how such a simple act had the potential to change her moment, her day and her world.

Grace knew life could never go back to what it once was and she wrote down and affirmed the words.

I Am awake, now!
I Am awake, now!
I Am awake, now!

Grace jumped out of bed with her now usual zest for life. She got dressed and headed off to see the old lady again. She had a very definite sense that a closure or completion was in the process of taking place.

Arriving at her destination she opened the large wooden door into her favourite garden. The little robin flew down as if to greet her, and then she watched, as he settled on the branch of a nearby conifer tree.

The house stood majestically beyond the lawn and the morning sunshine threw a golden seam of light around its edges. She adored it here. She followed the pebble path around the grass edge and onto the patio. As she approached she heard the voice from inside shout 'Come in.'

Grace entered to see the old lady sitting in one of the large leather chairs. She was writing, surrounded by a collection of what looked like small books. When Grace got closer she could see that they were not books at all but little journals. All sorts of shapes, sizes and colours. All of them well-worn and well-used. They were so pretty.

She picked up a rich purple and gold one, bound by a leather cord. She untied it and realising the text inside was hand written said 'Oh I am so sorry, how rude. I didn't realise this was your diary', and she quickly put it down.

'That's okay, Grace. It's not my diary. It's my Gratitude Journal. Here, I would love you to read it.' And the old lady picked it up and handed it back to Grace. 'Open it. Read it.'

Grace opened it again and began to read. The first entry was from January 1st, that year. It was written in the delicate spidery handwriting of an old person. She noticed that it was written in present tense. It read….

Thank you for this first day in what will be my most wonderful new year ever! I welcome it with open arms and know in my heart that this year will hold only the very best for me. I am so excited by the limitless possibilities that will be presented to me and I am grateful to receive yet another year of life's abundance. I choose to say YES to life and all of the inspiring and exciting adventures it will bring. My desires are flowing effortlessly to me and I love living my purpose. Thank you. Thank you. Thank you.

She continued to flick through. Each page was dated and it looked like there was an entry for each day of the year.

Grace picked pages quite randomly but each held a heart-felt and uplifting thankyou message. The little journal clearly charted a year in the life of someone who was glad to be alive.

Saturday 2nd February – Thank you for all the lovely birthday presents.
Friday 24th May - Thank you for helping me live from my heart and to trust my intuition.
Monday 3rd June - Thank you for answering all of my questions.
Friday 9th August -Thank you for helping me to see the best in people; to never gossip and to always forgive.
Wednesday 11th September - Thank you for the miracle of life. For my life and the lives of family and friends. Thank you for the truth.
Monday 17th September –Thank you for bringing Grace into my life.
Sunday 23rd September – Thank you for the precious gift that is my daughter.

Grace looked up at the old lady and gave her a loving smile. She felt so full of the emotions of gratitude and appreciation for what she was reading. It was extraordinarily beautiful.

'I have been writing these for years now. Here is my belief. There is always something to be grateful for, and if you can't find it, you're just not looking hard enough! When you make time to be grateful, you are celebrating all of the gifts in your life that can so easily slip away unnoticed. These little miracles are everywhere and have the potential to nourish and animate the wonder of your life. Most people let the precious moments of life pass them by, but with the practice of gratitude and celebration, we can lift our day, every day and fill it with the treasure of positive expectation and hope.'

Grace said eagerly. 'I wrote a thankyou message this morning. It wasn't anything I had learned. It just seemed a very natural thing to do, to acknowledge how much I appreciate having you in my life. But now that I know it is a "thing", I will make sure I do it deliberately every single day of my life. It's such a powerful idea. Thank you so much for sharing it with me.'

'You are very welcome, Grace. When the student is ready the teacher will appear.'

Grace loved this idea.

'We are nearly at the end of our adventures for now, but I still have a few things that I would like you to see. Quick, follow me.'

The old lady led Grace across the living space and into her bedroom. Grace instinctively took off her shoes as she entered and her feet sank into the thick wool pile carpet. Her feet tingled as they connected with the ground.

Grace paused astonished at the beauty that met her eyes. The room was magnificent, it took her breath away.

The old lady's clothes were housed behind immense glass doors. Everything was on display and the effect was stunning. Grace could see a glitzy gold and purple jump suit, a purple feather boa, a faux leopard-skin coat and an assortment of diamanté and sequined dancing shoes. Grace felt as if she had walked into a designer boutique in Paris.

A red crushed velvet headboard complemented a cashmere throw, embroidered with intricate sacred geometric designs.

One wall displayed a giant painting of a young Tibetan bride, whose magnificent multi-coloured head piece was fringed with droplets, each containing a semi-precious stone. Her skin was pale, her cheeks delicately pink and her beautiful almond eyes both innocent and mysterious. On the other wall hung a copy of the *Salvator Mundi,* elegantly mounted in an ornate silver gilt frame.

A large tear drop crystal chandelier hung from the ceiling's central cornice rose. Mini rainbows of light were thrown from the antique glass in every direction across the room.

Stained glass butterflies flitted across the large Victorian window. Outside Grace could see gigantic Japanese fir trees with plump wood pigeons nesting in their branches.

'This is the most gorgeous bedroom I have ever seen. Every little girl would want this, and every big girl too!'

'Yes, I love it myself. I am a very blessed' responded the old lady.

'But look at this' the old lady stood back and proudly pointed to a brightly coloured wall that looked oddly out of place. It was completely covered from floor to ceiling with a collage of images, inspiring words, maps of the world, keys, inventions, creations, stars, pictures of countries, young people, old people, the old lady herself, clothes, houses, cars, awards, memorabilia, feathers, famous celebrities, spiritual teachers, great leaders, spiraling galaxies, space crafts, glitter, money and cheques. The list was endless! What a magnificent masterpiece thought Grace.

'It's my "Vision Wall", Grace. Don't you just love it?' The old lady was clearly very proud of her vibrant creation.

'Your vision what?' said Grace astonished.

'My "Vision Wall." I started it many, many years ago. It was just a white painted wall back then. I decided to use it as a space to create a vision for my life.'

'Yes, but this takes vision to a whole new level!' said Grace and they both laughed.

'It has helped me deliberately create all the things I desire for myself or I should say, that life desires for me!'

'It's amazing. I would love to create my own one' Grace said in an excited voice. She then noticed something within the myriad of images and words. It was a book and it had her name on it.

'What is this?' and she pointed to the little Grace book image.

'It's a book I am writing. I believe it is now done.'

'Oh that's so exciting. Can I read it?'

'Not exactly. Not yet. It needs to be "downloaded" first.'

'Downloaded?' Grace was pretty confused.

'Yes, downloaded' she continued 'As you now know, everything starts with an intention or a desire. You then have to create a powerful image or a picture of the thing desired in your mind' said the old lady stretching her arms out in front of the book image on her vision wall and shouted 'Ta dah!'

'You then have to **Believe** that it is possible. **Believe** with all your heart. In fact you have to create an unshakeable belief that, from the very moment you set your intention, it is already done. You have to have faith that if your desire is in alignment with The Universe's desire for you, the only thing you need to do is be patient and allow it to be "downloaded" at exactly the right time and right place.'

'Oh! And just as important, you have to **Believe** that the right people will appear to help you!' The old lady then repeated the exact same 'Ta dah!' gesture, only this time more theatrically, with her arms outstretched towards Grace.

'The right people being…. me?' Grace pointed directly to her own chest. 'Are you talking about me?'

Grace was shell-shocked, completely unconvinced that she could possibly be "the one" for the job. There must be a million other people the old lady could have picked. Why me?

'Why not you?' the old lady asked as if reading her mind again.

'We are all chosen, Grace. We need only answer the call.'

'The question is… Do you believe? Do you have faith in yourself and your own ability, Grace? Do you believe that The Universe knows your purpose and gives you the perfect set of talents and gifts to fulfill your vision? Do you, Grace?'

'Do you believe that there are no coincidences in life and that The Universe conspired to bring us together?'

Grace stood looking down at her feet like a little girl, unsure of herself. Her teeth were clenched and she felt like crying.

'What is "yourself" telling you?' The old lady was pushing Grace for an answer. 'Your "self" **knows** what is right for you. Remember you just have to *Ask.*'

Grace closed her eyes and underneath her lids she looked up to the heavens. She inhaled and exhaled deeply several times. Squeezing the little rainbow pebble in her pocket, she asked, 'Is this my purpose? Is Grace, "The Book", my purpose?' She repeated the question over and over. Her body was shaking; her whole nervous system tingling.

There was complete silence and a gentle peace washed over her. Then from nowhere she felt a vibration *zip* past her right ear. It sounded like a voice. She recognised it from her visit to Leonardo's studio. It directed her gaze to the "Grace" book image on the wall, and said…'Yes, "Grace" is your purpose.'

Grace stood motionless. Everything felt perfect. She knew what she had been told was the truth.

As she opened her eyes a white peacock feather floated down through the air and brushed gently against her cheek. She stretched out to catch it, and as it landed on the palm of her hand, she smiled.

In that moment the words from a well-known verse popped into her mind. *Tuesday's child is full of Grace.*

Grace now knew with all of her heart that there was no coincidence between her name, her purpose, and the day on which she took her first breath on this beautiful planet; a Tuesday.

CHAPTER 22

THE INSTITUTE OF CREATION

Just as she wrote the final word in "The Book", Grace heard chimes from the grand-daughter clock in the hall. It was 12.00am, December 12th. She smiled as she laid her favourite pearl and gold leaf pen down beside "The Book." The download was complete. It was done.

It had taken her just under four weeks to write it. Impressive stuff for a novice author. Downloading must be a lot quicker now than it was in the old lady's day she giggled to herself.

It had also been nearly four weeks since she had seen the old lady. She had missed her. But she had been so busy with "The Book", writing it through the night whilst balancing her busy PR job.

She picked up "The Book" and flicked her fingers through the pages like a pack of cards. It was now full of beautiful handwritten words. Grace felt very proud.

'Well done, you. What an achievement!' Grace afforded herself some applause. The old lady had told her to find something to celebrate every day of her life and this was today's opportunity.

She pondered how the words had come to her so effortlessly. I suppose it is no surprise, in fact it was deliberate... Deliberate Creation.

Each night before she had begun to write a chapter, she performed a little ceremony. She lit a scented candle and played some peaceful music. She would then meditate on her Vision Wall, set clear intentions and *Ask* that the perfect words would flow easily through her. She would close her eyes and breathe gently as words, images and ideas streamed to her from the space where all possibilities exist. She knew this place, she had recently been there.

I have proven **The Creation Process**. "The Book" started as a blank sheet of paper. A space to create. I had a clear vision of my desire and I believed with all my heart that it was possible. I trusted that I was fulfilling my purpose and so it was created.

Grace knew the significance of this. She knew that if she was to bring this message to the world, then it was important that she could show it to be true.

Grace had a confidence about her. The kind of confidence that manifests as a result of setting out to do something and achieving it, when others in their unbelief thought it was impossible. Grace loved this new feeling.

She rose from her desk, walked across to the cupboard and opened it. She took out a roll of brown paper, some string and a pair of scissors. Perfect. I knew this was meant for something important she said to herself.

Grace picked up "The Book" and lightly kissed it. She closed her eyes and held it tight to her chest. She felt an immense surge of love emanate from "The Book", move through her heart and reach down to her toes. She visualised the waves of love spreading out at least eight to ten feet around her, hitting the walls of her bedroom and bouncing back, amplified by a million times.

She cut a square from the brown paper, carefully placed "The Book" in the centre and began to wrap it. Once sealed, she drew a large red heart on the front and remembering the old lady's words wrote *"Love is the supreme Creator."*

It is time, she thought, knowing that it was time to let "The Book" go back to its source; "The One" who had filled it with this precious knowledge.

Grace suddenly felt a little pang of anxiety, as the thoughts What about me? What will I do now? entered her mind. But, just as quickly, she recognised this as fear and she whispered 'I Am safe. I Am protected. I Am loved.' Instantly a peaceful calm cocooned her and all of her fears dissolved.

Grace went back to bed, deciding to catch a few hours sleep before it was really time to get up. She fell into a deep and peaceful unbroken slumber.

The alarm clock went off at its usual 5.55am, and Grace rolled over and dropped her feet down in search of her furry slippers.

It was a fine, crisp morning. The sun shone brightly and the winter frost glistened on the pavement and hedging like little sparkling diamonds. Grace loved the Christmas season and she knew that this year it was going to be extra special.

She waited happily at the bus stop. She had a strong feeling that this might be her final visit to the old lady for a while.

As she expected, the bus arrived perfectly on time. The bus driver gave her the loveliest smile and bid her a cheery good morning.

Grace smiled back saying, 'My journey is coming to an end. So we might not see each other for a while.'

The driver seemed to ignore what she was saying and instead said 'Did you know that her house was formerly a Carmelite Convent? Its beauty resides inside and out. Quite literally.'

She wasn't surprised that he knew the old lady, her inner beauty, and her house. Grace smiled gently whilst nodding in complete agreement.

She sat quietly looking out of the window and thought about her city. I love my city. There is so much going on. I suppose everyone's city is the same, if only people took the time to pause and really see.

As the bus approached its destination, Grace stood up ready to disembark. As she walked up to the driver's little cabin he gently took her arm, looked into her eyes and said 'It has been lovely meeting you. I have really enjoyed your company.'

He then surprised her completely by saying 'Can I have a signed copy when it's published? I like to read a good best seller!' and laughed his adorable laugh that Grace had become so fond of.

'Of course you can' Grace replied confidently, then hopped off the bus and waved him goodbye.

The old lady had requested that Grace meet her in her library today. It was situated at the back of the house. She made her way up a dramatic set of stone steps which were beautifully lit by a series of small black Victorian lanterns.

She reached the door and it opened automatically. Grace walked through and up the staircase crafted from rare Brazilian rosewood; obviously created in an age before the species had become endangered.

As she reached the top of the stairs, the old lady was standing waiting for her. Her outline was dwarfed by a life size stained glass window depicting a magnificent queen on a white horse. The queen was presiding over a victorious battle scene and being lauded by soldiers waving huge flags in celebration. As the sun shone through the window the old lady was surrounded by a rainbow aura.

'Hello, Grace. Welcome. So lovely to see you, my dear!' And she stretched both arms out to the full span of her tiny body and smiled from ear to ear.

'I love this building. There is something very special about it. She could sense legacy here. Grace thought about the woman wearing the tall plumed riding hat, who proudly watched over the entrance to the old lady's grand house and then said "there's a love story in this building, I can feel it."

'Come in. I am so pleased to see you again. How are you? Oh, we have so much to talk about' said the old lady.

They sat down on a comfy sofa and the old lady wrapped her cosy leopard print blanket around them both. How sweet thought Grace, realising that she had pre-heated it on the radiator for her arrival. 'I'm saving on my heating bills, these high ceilings cost a fortune, you know!' she giggled. Grace loved her little infectious laugh.

The two women chatted for a while, trading stories, drinking tea, eating cake and laughing lots. Suddenly the old lady jumped up and said 'I have a Christmas present for you. Here you are.'

'Oh, you didn't need to get me anything' said Grace surprised, but curious and eager to see what it was. She opened the beautifully packaged gift and pulled out the most exquisite fan made from peacock feathers. The colours of the silky feathers shone and shimmered in the sunlight. Grace held it up and leisurely fanned her face. There was something else in the package. It was a calendar for the New Year depicting exotic Indian princesses.

'Thank you. These gifts are so beautiful. Where did you get them?'

'I picked them up on a trip to India. They are handmade. The local people are so lovely there and very talented.'

Grace surveyed the room. She loved this library, the atmosphere was magical. She looked at the dark wooden bookcases, and now, knowing that it was previously a place where spiritual women had once lived, everything fell into place and made sense.

She looked at the bookcases again, old books comfortably battered, well-read and loved. This room was steeped in love. There were love hearts and keys dangling from the bookcase doors.

Grace realised that the old lady was looking at her. 'I'm sorry, I was lost in thought' she said.

The old lady laughed and patted Grace's hand, drawing the leopard print blanket tight around them.

'Oh, I nearly forgot, I've got something for you too' said Grace. She bent down and reached into her bag feeling for the brown paper parcel.

'I hope you like it.' She looked at the old lady rather nervously, trying to gauge her reaction.

'Is this what I think it is?' the old lady was thrilled and clasped her hands.

'Yes. It is.' Grace felt reassured.

The old lady took the parcel and read the words on the front of the paper. She took a sharp intake of breath and then turned to Grace saying 'That's beautiful, you remembered.' Unwrapping the it, she carefully lifted "The Book" out and held it tightly in both hands. She closed her eyes as if sensing the contents. She pressed it to her chest for quite a while, breathing very slowly.

Grace sat quietly and watched. She could feel her heart beating against her rib cage. The old lady opened her eyes and looked lovingly at "The Book." She then ran her fingers over its cover, and her big brown eyes welled up with tears. Finally she spoke. Her voice was barely a whisper. 'Thank you, Grace. I have waited such a long time for this. Finally my work here is done.'

The air in the library was still as if locked in a vacuum... nothing moved. Anticipation filled the air. Grace could feel it. Something was about to happen. Something amazing was about to take place.

The old lady finally opened "The Book's" cover. Immediately, light exploded from the pages, as if magic was being released into the air. They both drew breath. "The Book" had its own energy source; a glowing light that became stronger and stronger.

Grace's eyes widened. The light illuminated the old lady's face and Grace knew "The Book" had found its rightful owner. It was where it should be.

She was here to download "The Book" for the old lady. It was for her. In that moment Grace knew that they had both fulfilled their purpose and her heart sang with joy.

"The Book's" glow intensified. An image was materialising on the front cover, just beside the title "Grace". It was as if it was being drawn in small brush strokes by an invisible artist. The two women were captivated.

Finally the image was complete. A painting of an elegant peacock with a fan of snow white feathers presented itself. Grace thought that the exquisite bird perfectly embodied the name "Grace." The old lady looked at it and smiled, as if expecting to see it there.

Grace sensed something else. This wasn't the end, it wasn't finished. "The Book" had a destiny that was much, much bigger than the two women. 'Grace, we must now complete the circle. The wisdom we have been gifted, now held within the pages of "The Book", must be shared.'

The old lady stood up and began to speak in riddles.

'Whosoever is gifted this treasure,
filled with loving verse.
Holds in their hand The Key
that unlocks all of Creation
and the heart of The Universe.'

'But wait. There is another part to the rhyme. This is important' said the old lady.

'But be like a child, with a childlike heart,
for the message you wish to receive,
comes not from without but is found deep within
and is seen only by those who Believe.'

Grace was stunned by what she was hearing.

The old lady then began to flick furiously through the pages of "The Book." 'The Key ...within? ...within where? There must be something inside.' The two women then grinned at each other in amazement as the old lady discovered a little pocket in the back cover, and inside it, was a tiny key.

Grace looked at it, wide-eyed 'Had The Key been there all along?' Surely she would have seen it?'

The energy around the room was electric. She felt dizzy.

The old lady looked at her. 'There is one final thing that needs to be done, Grace.' And with that she bent down and picked up The Key. She held it out directly in front of her as she moved towards the central bookcase. It had clearly not been opened in many years. The books looked like they were in a deep sleep but the bookcase was slowly waking, simply by the old lady's presence.

She stood in front of it with "Grace" in one hand and "The Key" in the other. For a split second Grace saw her as a young woman with blonde hair, a happy smile and a steady gaze. Youthful and full of energy, a woman with a purpose, a purpose now fulfilled. A quiet calmness settled over the room and the old lady took a deep breath. She held up The Key and pressed it to her lips. As she placed it in the lock of the bookcase the door immediately flew open. Blinding rays of light burst through the doors along with a wind that knocked Grace off her feet and on to the ground.

Amazingly the old lady, slight as she was, was still standing. Grace watched as the light beamed all over the room, bouncing from wall to wall.

She was convinced she could feel the eyes of the authors, poets, saints, painters, and inventors burrow through the walls and stare down on them.

Grace stood up and walked towards the old lady. They peered into the open bookcase filled with old books from top to bottom.

But there was a space. A void. It was a space for one more book. Grace immediately knew. She screamed in excitement. 'It is this book! This is the one. The missing book!'

Just then, the old lady stepped forward and with a steady hand placed "The Book" in the space on the shelf. It fitted perfectly. 'You are home' she said in a soft motherly voice.

Instantly the whole room began to move and shake. The library was trembling. Everything in the room was coming alive. A wind howled and lights sparked. Grace's hair whipped across her face and she shielded her eyes from the light. She fought to balance herself as magnificent vibrations shook the building. It felt as if a new world was being created.

The old lady stood in the middle of it all. Her eyes closed. Her hands were high above her head, directed up towards the heavens. Surrounded by a rainbow of light, it was as if she was orchestrating the complete event. A flash of flame shot across the air towards the bookcase. And then, as if in response to an unheard silent command, everything began to slow down. Within a few seconds everything became calm and still.

The old lady opened her eyes and looked at Grace. 'Are you okay?' she asked. Grace was speechless and nodded, still holding her breath.

The old lady looked around as if seeing the room for the first time. Grace followed her gaze. At the top of the bookcase, Grace could see a flame dying out. In its wake she could see words branded into the charred wood. Four beautiful words.

It read "*The Institute of Creation.*"

Grace stumbled over to where the old lady stood, weeping.
'This is a thing of great beauty, Grace. I have waited all my life to create this place. I have been truly graced.'

Graces heart was pounding as she watched little tears flow from the old lady's beautiful brown eyes and drop onto her delicate rose coloured cheeks. She felt an abundance of grace abound from deep within her own heart.

'This is a space where spirit, philosophy and science meet as one. This Institute is "The Zeitgeist". It will capture the spirit of the age, the spirit of the time. Now is the right time for such a place.'

They both stood still, staring at the words. Finally the old lady broke the silence. 'But there is a final part to that riddle, Grace.'

'What riddle?' but then she remembered what the old lady had told her just before this whole incredible event.

'Ah, yes, that's it' continued the old lady.

'Whosoever writes the first,
will find their work is still undone.
For the message is timeless,
but its power is now.
For a new generation of hearts
still to be won.'

She then turned to Grace. 'Look at the books in the bookcase. Really look at them, Grace. Remember nothing is ever as it seems.'

Grace did as she was told. Slowly and carefully she began pulling them off the shelf. One by one she opened them to discover that they were all blank. Turning to the old lady with a shocked expression she said, 'They are all empty. Hundreds and hundreds of blank pages!'

'No, Grace. They are unwritten. They are waiting for intention and desire to spark them into life, to fill their pages with inspired words and images. They are waiting to be born in love, to be set free into the world, bringing Faith and Hope to those whose time it is to read them.'

'Remember how it all starts, Grace?' said the old lady. 'It starts with a blank page. A space to create. It's up to us, and many others, to take these pages and create a masterpiece.'

The old lady threw her arms up in the air and heralded 'The Institute of Creation is open.' And she laughed that infectious laugh that Grace loved.

EPILOGUE

G race looked down at the words "The Key" on the tiny luminous screen on her mobile phone, as it vibrated in her hand. She felt excited and, if the truth be told, extremely nervous. She chatted happily for a few minutes with the woman at the other end of the phone and then hung up.

Walking down the hall, she passed the grand-daughter clock on the way, pausing to look at her face in the burnished framed mirror before leaving. She smiled at herself and said aloud, '**I Am** a confident speaker and a bestselling author.' She giggled like a little girl as she closed the door of her flat behind her.

Her emotions intensified as she waited for the bus and its driver to arrive. She hadn't seen him in such a long time. As she hopped on, she was greeted warmly as the driver reached right across from his seat and hugged her tightly. 'I told you you would do it. I am so proud of you' he said. Grace felt pure joy emanate from his very soul.

She told him her new destination, and the driver agreed to take her on her little detour "off piste" as he called it. She admired his sense of adventure and his courage.

Grace sat down and gazed dreamily out of the window. She felt a huge sense of pride as she passed many well-known sites in her city. The bus stopped and as she made her way off she reached into her bag for the little brown paper parcel. 'Here you go. As promised' she said as she handed it over.

The driver took the package in both hands and held it close to his heart. 'Thank you, Grace. I will cherish this forever' he said with a choked voice and tears in his eyes.

Grace stepped off the bus and into a beautiful bright, summer sunshine day. The Stadium stood directly in front of her. It was a magnificent piece of architecture. A gigantic muti-coloured glass spaceship, sitting on its curved launch pad, all ready for lift off.

Grace walked nervously across the decorated concrete plaza and towards the large and impressive entrance. Her heart pounded like a giant steel drum. As she entered, she was stopped in her tracks. She took several seconds to steady herself, as emotion began to well up from deep inside. She had to do everything in her power to hold back her tears.

Lining the foyer, were two rows of gigantic, colourful banners. They towered ten feet high above her. Grace immediately recognised the happy, confident faces. Vibrant men and women. "The Key" teachers smiled at her from below enormous "Key" logos. She stopped for a moment and took time to read the words written in silver and black, boldly promoting "The Key Weekend Experience." Another surge of pride shot through her entire body.

However mesmerising these images were, it was the banners on the end of the last two rows that captured Grace's attention and took her breath away. She looked at them, gasping in awe and amazement. The banners proclaimed, "Grace - The Book", written in gold, across the top. The most beautiful photo of Grace and the old lady filled the rest of the space below. The two women looked so happy and were laughing and hugging each other, clearly having the time of their lives. Grace pinched herself, she could not quite take in the enormity of what she was experiencing. Grace had written a book with the old lady, Founding Teacher of "The Key", a philosophy that was now awakening and energising the world.

She was suddenly distracted as a young man walked toward her.

'Hello, Grace. You are very welcome here' he said with a huge grin which revealed shiny metal braces on his perfectly white teeth. He had a shock of red unruly hair and a face full of freckles. He shook her hand firmly 'We are all waiting for you. The programme session is just about to finish and then you will be on.'

Grace felt a tidal wave of energy, like an electric shock, pass through her. It started in her stomach and finished in her heart; it hurt a little. The young man touched Grace's arm gently, looked at her with knowing eyes and said 'Don't worry, all is well. Come this way.' He then led her past a row of tables, with snowy white table cloths, stacked high with her "Grace" books. Grace felt yet another surge of pride as she looked at the beautiful cover. The memory of the white peacock drawing itself onto "The Book" in the library flashed through her mind in an instant.

Taking her arm, the young man guided her along a brightly lit corridor, lined with even more images of the smiling "CelebriKey" teachers that she had seen on the banners outside.

They stopped at the stage door. Grace felt dizzy and faint. She closed her eyes and began to breathe slowly and deliberately to relax herself. She started repeating the now familiar words.

'**I Am** a confident speaker and bestselling author.'
'**I Am** a confident speaker and bestselling author.'
'**I Am** a confident speaker and bestselling author.'

As she opened her eyes she suddenly realised the floor was vibrating, it was positively bouncing. She could hear the sound of the stadium mega speakers blasting out music, as people shouted, sang, cheered and celebrated. The energy was palpable.

The young man opened the door and helped Grace up the steep wooden stairs. He then stopped her at a set of navy blue velvet curtains, which lined the stage on either side from top to bottom.

It was then that Grace caught her first glimpse of the little old lady. But she was not alone. She was surrounded by a group of loving and supportive people. Grace recognised most of them. A beautiful older woman with strawberry blond hair, with a beauty that reached deep into her soul, stood at the old lady's right hand side. There was a stunning young woman, who stood to the old lady's left. Grace now recognised her as the old lady's daughter. She represented The Key New Generation. And then there was "The Key" teacher whom Grace had spoken to earlier that morning. They had eventually met after that fated day when she had taken the wrong bus. Behind them stood a large group of vibrant "Key People".

Grace now knew that she truly belonged.

She turned her attention to the old lady who looked radiant with her hair tied back and off her face. She was wearing an all-in-one purple and gold jump suit, topped off with a purple ostrich feather jacket, which sat neatly on her delicate waist. Gold strappy sandals adorned her tiny feet. Grace could see a platinum and diamond key hanging from a long chain around her neck. As the necklace caught the stadium lights, it created a dazzling kaleidoscope of colour, which bounced off the old lady and across the whole stage.

The old lady spotted Grace. Holding the microphone to her mouth she announced. 'My wonderful "Key People", will you please give a warm welcome and a standing ovation to Grace, our very own award winning, bestselling author.'

Grace's knees began to tremble and her whole body shook. She thought she would collapse, but just then, the young man pushed her shoulders gently and suddenly she found herself standing out on stage.

Grace gazed out from the stage into an infinite universe of twinkling lights. Her eyes were met with a whirlpool galaxy of smiling faces. The auditorium was circular and with its array of sophisticated flash and strobe lighting, she imagined she was on the bridge of an enormous intergalactic spacecraft. Grace looked up, and was completely astonished by the beauty of the light system suspended from the stadium roof. The lights were laid out in a mesmerising and precise sequence. The whole sparkling effect spiraled like a giant conch shell or the swirling seeds at the centre of a sunflower. She was speechless and could find no words to describe the divine vision.

Grace surveyed the scene. Everything was in slow motion. Although she could see the mouths of the crowd shouting, she could not hear their words. She was cocooned in a still, peaceful silence. It felt totally surreal. Suddenly her attention was drawn to two people in the heart of the crowd. Grace could not believe her eyes. It was her mother and father. They stood together beaming with pride. A tidal wave of emotion rushed though her heart and flooded her eyes with tears.

The old lady advanced towards her. The noise and frenzy of the crowd tumbled back into her world. She grabbed her with that uncanny strength of hers and hugged her tight to her chest. Grace immediately felt calm. As the two women embraced, a faint tendril of green energy flowed from their hearts and surrounded their bodies.

The old lady looked lovingly into Grace's eyes and leaning closer, whispered into her ear 'Grace, this is your moment, be present and enjoy it.' She then stepped back to allow Grace centre stage.

Grace's hands were shaking uncontrollably as she began to read from her own copy of The Grace Book. It was now lovingly well used. She had tiny coloured stickers scattered throughout its pages, carefully marking all of her favourite parts.

You could hear a pin drop as Grace began to read her prologue.

'It was said that "The Book" would be found in darkest space; in a void where all possibilities exist. It was waiting there to be created. Waiting for "the one" to imagine it into reality.

A talisman to be passed from age to age, from mother to daughter and from father to son, an institute for the generations still to come. "The Book" contained "The Key." The Key that unlocks all of Creation and the heart of The Universe itself.

A precious treasure, "The Book" had been desired by many. But even those who had held it in their hand could not see the power that lay within, for it was the simplicity of its message that fooled them, and their chosen unbelief.

But a child could see it. A child-like heart would understand its simple message.'

Like a tiny Alice in Wonderland, Grace stood on the enormous stage reading selected extracts from "The Book". The massive gathering was spellbound as they listened. As she finished her reading, there was complete and uninterrupted silence. Then, a deafening cheer erupted, and the audience rose as one, and thousands of hands applauded.

In that exact moment, Grace knew they had understood the meaning of *the word*.

WITH GRATITUDE TO

AVRIL CADDEN

I met Avril at a Key event and spoke to her about my desire to create "The Book". We spent a magical year together talking about ideas and inspirations and drafting the framework for what is now Grace. I am very grateful for your beautiful mind and your valued contribution, which I believe was a key element in the creation process. With love and admiration for you Avril.

ANNE MCINTOSH

Anne, my treasured friend. I will be eternally grateful for your unshakeable belief in me and in Grace. Your work in the final stages of Grace's development was considerable and invaluable, and I believe helped me lift Grace up to the little masterpiece that it has become.

MEGAN MCGRORY

I often describe you as my best creation ever! You are a source of pure love and joy in my life. I am so happy and proud that you have chosen to take our message to The Key New Generation, fulfilling the promise in the Prologue and last chapter of Grace. I love you to the end of The Universe and beyond Megan, my beautiful daughter.

My Family

With love and gratitude to my mum and dad. I hope that I am one of your best creations ever. I live to make you proud, and I love you now, until eternity. To Laura my beautiful sister, and John, for your kindness and support when I needed it. To my amazing brothers Tony and Paul, your beautiful wives and all of your own magical little creations, I love you all dearly. Thank you Paul for asking me *why?* and for your marketing pearls of wisdom.

'Key Auntie' Frances

Thank you Frances for your love and support. You are a Key treasure, not only to me, but to all of The Key People Community that you have also lovingly supported.

Katherine Murray

Katherine, you were there taking care of me at our first Key event together. Thank you for always listening and saying exactly the right things, at exactly the right time. I miss and love you very much.

Dawn Gibbins MBE

Dawn, thank you for being the sunshine spirit that you are. For embracing me and The Key, and for your generous heart. You believed in me and my dreams and gave me the start I needed to bring The Key to the world.

Lauren Taylor, Founding Key Franchisee

Like the trailblazers in Chapter 12, The Spirit of Adventure, you were prepared to trust and venture into the unknown. As a result we are now creating a world of magical possibility together. Thank you.

VALERIE KERR

Thank you for the courage to come with me (and all of our future Key Teachers) on a magical journey, teaching The Key across the planet, both by land and by sea!

LILIA SINCLAIR

With much gratitude to you Lilia for your support and belief in The Key. You're are a true "Keyliever".

KAREN LARTER, EDITOR

I give thanks for the day that you walked into my life, delivered to me from heaven, to guide us and bring Grace home "word perfectly". You arc an important and inspirational lady.

ROBERT CLARK

Thank you for deepening my understanding of *grace* and for your incredible service to me and priceless contribution to designing "The Book" cover.

DR. NIGEL WOOD, GRAHAM MCNEIL & HELEN MCLAUGHLIN

Thank you for reading and reviewing Grace, for your important input and invaluable recommendations. Supreme team!

KEY AMBASSADORS & KEY PEOPLE

To all of the amazing Key Ambassadors & Key People .I am truly grateful to each and everyone one of you. Special thanks to Kirsteen, Andy, Eleanor, Chrissy, Elaine, Shona, Michelle, Bev, Des, Wendy, Jackie, Wesley and Paul.

MELISSA, MADDIE & HAZEL

Thank you girls for being the first young people to read and critique Grace. Your words and wonderful ideas gave me so much encouragement and hope that Grace would go out into the world and delight a new generation.

ABOUT THE AUTHOR

CHRISTINE FRIEL MCGRORY MSC. BSC.

Christine is a successful entrepreneur, an inspired speaker and corporate trainer within many of the UK's top 100 companies. She is widely recognised for her charm, grace and unique ability to engage the heart.

Practising and teaching a variety of transformational leadership and spiritual approaches learned from world-class teachers, and with a MSc. in Corporate Leadership and a BSc in Chemistry, Christine is uniquely positioned to understand and teach both the spirit and science behind Creation.

Receiving recognition from the Queen in 2000 for her work in the community, she has also been voted one of Scotland's most influential women.

In 2010, Christine's entrepreneurial spirit unlocked "The Key"; a seminal personal transformation programme. With her unique creative ability, Christine has now authored "Grace" which takes The Key Philosophies and winds them into a ground breaking, magical and powerful life changing story.

www.gracethekeybook.co.uk.
Email : create@unlock-the-key.co.uk
www.unlockthekey.com

ABOUT THE ARTIST

GILLIAN ORR B.A.(HONS)

Gillian is a talented multi-media artist. A graduate of the prestigious Glasgow School of Art, Gillian's enviable skills base comprises a wide range of disciplines including, fashion, textiles and prop design.

Her work has appeared in many diverse formats throughout the country ranging from extensive festival murals to intimate exhibitions of her own personal collection.

Gillian has a particular interest and belief in the therapeutic nature of art, creativity and the design process.

Christine is both delighted and honoured that Gillian accepted her invitation to design the artwork for Grace's book cover, 'Creation.'

Email : orrgillian@yahoo.co.uk
www.unlockthekey.com/grace

ABOUT THE KEY

The Key® teaches The Creation Process® a genius three-step process which equips you with the "know how" and the tools to create whatever it is you want and desire in your life. Created from a series of powerful ancient and timeless philosophies, The Key deepens your awareness of you, your environment, and your world. The Key is the spirit of NOW.

Christine Friel McGrory unlocked "The Key" in 2010. She now delivers The Key Experience, comprising; The Key Weekend training courses, Unlock® Mentoring, Vision Workshops, The Key Corporate Leadership Programme, and The Key to Health & Wellbeing; all taught by Christine and her hand-picked Key Teachers through a unique Franchise network across the UK.

Christine's daughter, Megan, is now teaching The Key New Generation to young people in schools, colleges and workplaces across Scotland.

For more information about The Key Franchise, The Key Weekend Courses, The Key Corporate, The Key New Generation and The Key to Health & Wellbeing.

Visit: www.unlockthekey.com.
Email: create@unlock-the-key.co.uk
www.gracethekeybook.co.uk.
www.theinstituteofcreation.org

THE KEY®
TO WEALTH, HEALTH & HAPPINESS

THE INSTITUTE
OF CREATION

The Institute of Creation was opened in 2014. The purpose of the Institute is to create a sense of belonging and to empower people with the resources that will allow them to live an abundant, happy, healthy, purposeful and fulfilled life.

The Institute of Creation teaches The Key Programme and aims to support wider access to the following individuals and groups.

Those who:

- are unemployed and have a desire to improve their circumstances.
- are recovering from addictions or other life challenges, live in areas of deprivation but aspire to better their and their families' lives.
- have learning difficulties and/or who wish to engage in creative activity.
- are children and young people who have disengaged from education.
- are recovering from ill health, and who wish to take control of their own health and well-being, and create a brighter, healthier future
- have retired, but still feel that they have a life to live and a valued contribution to make to society.
- who have experienced family trauma, and wish to gain more confidence.

For more information: www.theinstituteofcreation.org
To donate, email: philanthropy@theinstituteofcreation.org

FURTHER READING

1. The Holy Bible
2. Opening Doors Within : Eileen Caddy
3. Journey to Self Realisation : Paramahansa Yoganandi
4. A Course in Miracles : Foundation for Inner Peace
5. Conversations with God : Neale Donald Walsh
6. Deepak Chopra : SynchroDestiny
7. Ask And It Is Given : Abraham Hicks
8. Frequency : Penny Pierce
9. You Can Heal Your Life : Louise Hay
10. The Biology of Belief : Bruce Lipton
11. The Secret Life of Your Cells : Robert.B.Stone
12. The Science of Being Great : Wallace.D.Wattles
13. The Overview Effect: Space Exploration and Human Evolution
14. The Pursuit of Purpose : Myles Munro
15. The Divine Matrix : Greg Braden
16. Awareness : Neville
17. Three Magic Words : Uell. S. Anderson
18. The I AM Discourses : St Germaine
19. The Chronicles of Narnia : C. S. Lewis
20. The Famous Five and The Secret Seven : Enid Blyton
21. www.heartmath.org
22. www.theinstituteofcreation.org